The Rylee Adamson Epilogues, Book 2

PRAISE FOR THE RYLEE ADAMSON NOVELS

"Shannon Mayer's Rylee Adamson paranormal romances keep me glued to the page. Rylee is a kick-ass character who loves with her whole heart and reminds me of my own Rose Gardner—a collector and protector of lost and broken souls. Every new book is better than the last and I always finish her latest book hungry for more."

-Denise Grover Swank
New York Times and USA Today Bestselling Author

"The Rylee Adamson Novels are filled with a wonderfully detailed and rich paranormal world with engaging characters, a fast paced plot and lots of action. A must read for urban fantasy lovers."

-Eve Langlais
New York Times and USA Today Bestselling Author

"If you love the early Anita Blake novels by Laurel K. Hamilton, you will fall head over heels for The Rylee

Adamson Series. Rylee is a complex character with a tough, kick-ass exterior, a sassy temperament and morals which she never deviates from. She's the ultimate heroine. Mayer's books rank right up there with Kim Harrison's, Patricia Brigg's, and Ilona Andrew's. Get ready for a whole new take on Urban Fantasy and Paranormal Romance and be ready to be glued to the pages!"

-Just My Opinion Book Blog

Copyright
LIAM (The Rylee Adamson Epilogues, Book 2)

Original Cover Art by Damon Za
Mayer, Shannon

USA Today Bestselling Author

SHANNON
MAYER

The Rylee Adamson Epilogues, Book 2

ALSO BY SHANNON MAYER

The Rylee Adamson Novels

Priceless (Book 1)
Immune (Book 2)
Raising Innocence (Book 3)
Shadowed Threads (Book 4)
Blind Salvage (Book 5)
Tracker (Book 6)
Veiled Threat (Book 7)
Wounded (Book 8)
Rising Darkness (Book 9)
Blood of the Lost (Book 10)
Alex (A Short Story)
Tracking Magic (A Novella 0.25)
Elementally Priceless (A Novella 0.5)
Guardian (A Novella 6.5)
Stitched (A Novella 8.5)

The Rylee Adamson Epilogues

RYLEE (Book 1)
LIAM (Book 2)
PAMELA (Book 3)

The Elemental Series

Recurve (Book 1)
Breakwater (Book 2)
Firestorm (Book 3)
Windburn (Book 4)
Rootbound (Book 5)
Ash (Book 6)

The Blood Borne Series
(Written with Denise Grover Swank)

Recombinant (Book 1)
Replica (Book 2)

The Nevermore Trilogy

The Nevermore Trilogy
Sundered (Book 1)
Bound (Book 2)
Dauntless (Book 3)

A Celtic Legacy

A Celtic Legacy
Dark Waters (Book 1)
Dark Isle (Book 2)
Dark Fae (Book 3)

The Risk Series
(Written as S.J. Mayer)

High Risk Love (Book 1)

Contemporary Romances
(Written as S.J. Mayer)

Of The Heart

CHAPTER 1

THE DAYS BEFORE the triplets fell ill were quiet, so quiet, without Rylee there and nothing but thoughts of her haunting my restless sleep. Wondering if she would come back, and if so, in what condition? Would the fear that hid behind her eyes be wiped away, or would it have burrowed in like a parasite that would change her forever?

Kav, Bam, and Rut had seemed to pick up on my worry, as they were increasingly quiet, sleeping longer, playing less. All of my concerns had made me a fool not to see that the triplets were growing pale, and I'd let Louisa's words of calm reassurance make me ignore my instincts.

I knew something was wrong, and yet I'd kept my blinders on. Hoping I was mistaken, that I was seeing things that weren't there . . . but I hadn't been.

The new recruits Rylee had brought with her, Belinda and Levi, siblings with a hint of elemental blood in them, had gone with Rylee to get groceries and that's when it happened. Almost as if the triplets had been waiting for Rylee. With her home, it was as if a light switch had flicked off within the triplets and they went downhill in a matter of a single hour.

Almost as if they knew I wouldn't have noticed, so caught up as I was in my worry for her.

So they waited for their mother to be near, knowing she

would save them. Knowing she was the one who would find the cure to their mysterious illness.

And then Rylee had sent me after the one thing that *could* save the babies. A female ogre, one willing to be a wet nurse for three babies.

I ran for my weapons in our bedroom, listening to Rylee give orders, listened to her call Doran and her grandparents to come and help her. I grabbed a bag from the closet and shoved in several knives, and a thick woolen coat. There wasn't much else that would do me any good.

I looked around the room, breathing the space in.

Sending Rylee away on a salvage brought her back to me whole, at peace with her own nature. For her to stay home with the babies and send me on my own, I wondered . . . did she see the fear in my own eyes? I shook my head. No, I knew she hadn't. I'd done everything I could to keep it from her. To give her the space she needed without her having to deal with me and my shit.

I slung the bag over my shoulder and ran through the house. Rylee had Kav in her arms. His eyes were closed and his heart beat at an unsteady rate. I didn't stop, though, not even to kiss them all goodbye. Because I knew that if I thought about the triplets dying, I wouldn't be able to move, I would freeze in place and hold them as if my love alone would save them.

If I stopped now, I wouldn't be able to do what I had to do.

Time to put all the emotional shit on the back

burner and get the job done. Time to put back on the visage of an FBI agent on a case.

Hurry, Liam . . . hurry.

Rylee's words echoed in my ears as I ran along the driveway and jumped into the new Jeep I'd bought her only a week before. I jammed the keys in the ignition and turned them. Nothing. The engine made a vain attempt at a rumble that sounded more like it was laughing at me than actually trying to turn over. "Piece of shit." I slammed my hands on the wheel, cursing my own stupidity. More than any other supernaturals, I tended to have that kind of effect on technology, shutting it down by just being within a ten-foot proximity.

Just another curse of being a Guardian who'd taken over a vampire's body, I suppose. I shuddered, my skin all but crawling with the need to get away from itself. This was not the time to consider the fact that my body was not my own. That I had basically become a body snatcher. That I was no longer the man I once was, that the mirror didn't show me a face I knew other than as someone I'd hated.

Something I would deal with another time.

Maybe.

Or maybe I'd just ignore it and hope it stopped bothering me. Yeah, that sounded like the way to go. Stuff those thoughts as deeply as I could, away from the front of my brain where they would do nothing but distract me from the task at hand.

A task I refused to think about failing.

I jumped out of the Jeep and slammed the door hard enough to bend it inward. I didn't really know why I'd even tried the new one other than the fact that I'd bought it for Rylee to replace the old clunker she'd been driving for years. I thought, stupidly, that a new toy would help draw her out of her head, help her see that there were still good things in the world.

That she was one of those good things.

It hadn't worked.

And now, I had no choice but to take said clunker with its multitude of dents, bangs, and bent rims. With a leap, I slid across the hood of the new Jeep, scratching it, my bag of weapons and extra clothes dragging behind me. In seconds, I was in Rylee's black, beat-up hunk of metal. The seat sagged under my weight and I shifted it backward to accommodate my long legs. Longer than before. I shook my head, not for the first time getting hung up on the details of my new body.

"Liam, wait!"

I twisted in my seat and stared at the kid running out the door. Levi was tall and gangly like so many teenage boys who hadn't found their stride yet, who hadn't started to fill out. His messy brown hair and light brown eyes reminded me of Alex. He stumbled on the bottom step as he yanked a heavy winter coat on. He had a woven cap he pulled down over his ears. Like he was going somewhere. "I . . . I'm coming with you."

Oh, this was not happening. The kid wanted to

help. I could appreciate that. But not today, not on this run.

"No, you're not." I turned my back on him and rolled up the window without even considering his request. The kid had only been with us a few days, and while I knew he was a good kid, he wasn't really a supernatural. He was a half-breed elemental that could barely touch his abilities. Or maybe he couldn't touch them at all, which made him just a body to be in the way. Cannon fodder on a good day. The other part of it was he was far from solid in another way—his past had broken him from what Rylee had told me, making him an unknown when it came to a crisis or scenario that would require snap decisions and bold thinking. I only knew a little bit about the abuse he and his sister had suffered at the hands of their father, but I didn't need to know more.

I'd seen it with too many kids on the streets, the perpetual hunch in the shoulders, the flinch of muscles if you made a move toward them. The darting eyes. They weren't shady; they were like dogs that had been beaten down, chained and starved. There would come a point where the break would happen and either he would lash out, or totally fold in on himself. I couldn't afford for either to happen on this job.

He didn't slow down. "Rylee said I should come with you." I could hear him even with the doors shut and the windows rolled up. Wolf ears were incredibly strong even when I was in human form. Not that I'd been able to shift since I'd been in Faris's body.

Again, a problem for another day.

Not today.

Levi hurried to the other side of the Jeep as he zipped up his coat against the constant blowing wind here in North Dakota. "She says she has a feeling you're going to need me. And maybe you're going to need this." He opened the door and let himself in as he held up a cell phone attached to a long cord. He plugged the cord into the lighter.

A cell phone. Damn, that *was* a good idea. There was no way I could handle a cell phone without it shutting down on me within seconds of touching it. This would give me access to Rylee. I could get information to and from her without trying to find a land-line, something that was becoming increasingly more difficult.

I bit back the words that spilled up my throat and then swallowed them. If Rylee wanted him to come, there was a reason, more than just the cell phone. Even I was smart enough to know that. I trusted her more than I trusted myself some days, so it looked like Levi was coming along for the ride. I locked down the irritation of my tagalong.

"Fine. Get in. But you do what I say, when I say it. This is no Sunday drive to Grandma's house, and I can't be pulling your ass out of the fire, got it?"

He nodded and shut the door on the passenger side of the Jeep, his face a careful blank. From what I knew of his father, Levi had learned to deflect a lot of abuse, verbal and physical. But I didn't have time to feel bad for laying the truth out. The kid had to get used to things done my way. And I had to hope he didn't melt down along the way.

I stuck the key into the ignition and threw my bag of weapons into the backseat.

The engine rolled over with a thick grumble that sounded like at least two pistons were sticking, and a third ready to blow up. Again. I shook my head and backed out of the driveway so quickly, the Jeep rocked on two wheels for a moment.

Levi gripped the armrest on the door, his eyes shut tightly. But he didn't say anything.

I slammed the Jeep into drive and hit the gas. We needed to get to the farm on the outskirts of Bismarck as fast as possible.

The ogre tribe that Rylee had seen, the first and only ogres we'd run into in the six months since the battle with Orion, had been in Seattle.

Taking a flight to Seattle was an option, but only if I managed to not cause the plane's engines to fail. Something I'd done in the past. On top of that, between booking and waiting on a commercial flight, I was sure Ophelia could get me to Seattle faster, and today it was all about speed.

The fear that I was not going to make it in time to save the triplets roared up in me, rolling my stomach in one giant knot. I grimaced and drew in a slow breath. My training as an FBI agent kicked in hard, and I let it take over.

There was only one way I was managing this trip. Boxes.

I took my emotions and shoved them into a box

next to all the other fears hidden in the depths of my heart, locked it tightly and threw it to the back of my mind. Tasks were what I had, and what I would deal with. I focused on that and put the image of the babies away.

Slowly the fear left, replaced by a growing determination and a single goal set in a series of steps. But ultimately, it came down to one thing.

"So we're really going to an ogre tribe?" Levi asked.

I glanced at the kid. "We have one job, and one job only, and that is to find a female ogre. The ogre mob Rylee dealt with in Seattle is extremely territorial. They have humans working for them, and they kill any supernatural who shows up on their turf without question. From what she said, they are smarter than the average ogre too, or at least, they think they are."

From the corner of my eye, I saw Levi frown. "How are we going to convince them they should help us? I . . . I've found violent people aren't really prone to reason."

He had a very good point, one I'd seen over and over as an FBI agent. The more violent a person, the more buried they were in their own twisted logic. Snapping them out of it was rare. I didn't answer Levi right away because I didn't know the "how" of what we were doing, only that we were doing it. First step was to get to Seattle as fast as possible.

Convincing the ogre tribe to help would be no easy task. Then to further convince an ogre female to come back with us . . . I'd be begging the gods to help on this one. But without a female ogre, the ogre triplets would die. Their bodies shutting down as each second passed. That was not an outcome I was willing to consider, and again, I pushed those thoughts away.

"Mother Nature is a bitch, Levi. Just like some animals can't be fostered before a certain age, ogre babies are the same. Without the specific nutrients from an ogre mother's milk, the triplets will die. We aren't letting that happen, which means between here and Seattle, we're going to come up with a plan. There has to be at least one female ogre that would be maternal enough, and willing, to help."

He slowly nodded. "Okay, so we're really just going in on a hope and a prayer."

I ran a hand through my hair and glanced in the rearview mirror as I sped down the highway. "Yeah, something like that."

A hope and a prayer. That was Rylee's style, though to be fair, she usually involved more than a bit of sword swinging and f-bombs. That wasn't my style.

Even though I said I didn't have a plan, the seeds of one were sprouting. The quieter we were, the better. Slipping in on the outskirts of Seattle and keeping clear of the ogres until we scoped out the situation would probably be best.

Maybe we could cut one from the herd and do an interrogation.

I glanced at the speedometer. The farm was a couple hours away, and we were making it in record time.

The image of the three ogre babies, limp, unmoving, their normally colorful skin pale, and their tiny hands clenched as though in pain . . .

No.

My jaw tightened. I would not allow it to happen. They were my boys as much as Marcella was mine. As much as Zane was mine. I would fight with everything I had, down to my last breath, to save them.

"Um. Liam. The airport is the other way," Levi said.

"We aren't going via plane. Ophelia is going to help us."

"The dragon?" he blurted, excitement all over him like a puppy teased with a bright, shiny new toy.

I nodded. "Yes." I didn't elaborate that Ophelia was the reason I doubted I was going to need Levi's help. Dragons were naturally immune to magic, and they were as tough as they came. Though, it had been ogres who had taken out Blaz, Ophelia's mate and one of Rylee's closest friends. I had to believe she would be willing to help. She was, after all, a mother herself and bonded to Rylee so she knew what the ogre babies meant to her.

The highway was mostly vacant, dotted here and there with vehicles or the odd tractor moving like a plodding green or red speed bump.

I wove the Jeep around vehicles, and as beat-up as it was, the clunker was still responsive in handling.

Levi grunted as we skimmed next to a car. "Um, that's a bit close."

Two vehicles in front of us blocked the way, but I

didn't slow. That wasn't an option. I jerked the wheel hard to the right and hit the gas pedal, taking us up the shoulder, spitting gravel behind us. Levi's face paled. The gravel tugged at the Jeep, pulling it toward the deep ditch. I kept the wheel steady, muscles tense as I kept us from rolling over altogether.

Barely.

Signage for the posted speed limit raced toward us in our improvised driving lane. The space between the sign and the large truck on my left was going to be tight. I held the Jeep steady and kept the gas pedal down as far as it would go.

"Hang on, this will be close."

"Holy shit, man!" Levi yelled as we shot through the tight space, the Jeep's right side mirror ripping off against the sign pole with an audible tear and ting of metal on metal.

"Hold on to your panties," I said as we sped down the shoulder of the highway, finally passing the blockade. I pulled the wheel to the left, once more on the main road. I didn't look at Levi, but I could feel him staring at me.

"I thought you were a cop?" he breathed.

"FBI," I said. "Doesn't mean I won't break the law if I need to."

"Yeah. I've seen that before," he whispered. There was pain in those words I didn't like.

Which led me to the obvious next question. "Was your dad a cop?"

He shrugged and shook his head. He stared out the window, lost in whatever memories haunted him.

"No one believed us when we told them what he was doing to Belinda."

I kept still and let him talk. As if the floodgates had opened, the words poured out of him.

"They said he was one of the best police officers Bismarck had, and they wouldn't hear us bad-mouthing him because we were a couple of spoiled kids. He told them Belinda was a whore, that she was a druggie. That I was her pimp."

Anger sliced through me because I'd seen it before. Not just cops, but anyone in power who thought they could use their position to break the law and get what they wanted no matter who it hurt. I almost eased off on the gas pedal. Almost.

"I'm sorry. I didn't mean I would break the law like that. When someone you love is in danger . . . you will do anything to save them. No matter the cost."

He shrugged. "It doesn't matter now, Rylee fixed it. He never would have stopped, you know, what he was doing to little girls. He told me once, when he was drunk, he already had another girl picked out after Belly went missing."

It took me a moment to remember that Belly was Belinda. "Who did he have lined up?"

"There was a single mom across the street who was struggling to keep food on the table." He stared out the windshield. "He'd already been charming her. She had a ten-year-old daughter."

My guts churned with disgust and a slow-burning rage. I almost wished Rylee hadn't shot the bastard in the head, just so I could have the distinct pleasure of watching him piss his pants as I came at him in wolf form.

Levi shifted his weight in his seat, drawing my eyes to him.

For just a moment, it felt as though he was someone else. The image next to me wavered and it was if Alex sat beside me, not Levi. That did make me really look at him. Same brown hair, gangly build, but the eyes were wrong. Alex's eyes were never shuttered with past pain as Levi's were. His golden eyes had been full of nothing but love for his people and love for life despite what he'd seen. Alex had lost his sister and father, but it hadn't cut into him like it had Levi. Even after Alex had been able to fully shift, there had been no loss of that joy he carried in him.

Levi, on the other hand . . . he was so serious, it was hard to look at him for too long. Like he carried the weight of all he'd seen in his soul, and it spilled out his eyes, making you re-evaluate your own choices. Had you protected those around you enough? Had you stopped enough bad guys to make the world a better place? Or were you no better than them, breaking the law for your own cause?

I snorted at myself. I was starting to sound like my grandfather with his words of wisdom that usually made sense too late, far beyond the time they could've been helpful.

"Liam?"

"Yeah?"

"I think maybe you shouldn't have broken the

law," Levi said. I wanted to smack my head on the steering wheel.

"Look, kid, there's a time and place, and this is one of those times the law is in the way of saving lives—"

"No, I mean, look behind us." Levi twisted in the seat, and I checked the rearview mirror.

Behind us, a set of flickering police lights shattered the growing darkness of the late afternoon. No siren, though.

I glanced at my speedometer, already knowing a ticket was warranted but not giving a shit how many tickets I was given. The thing was, I knew I could outdrive whoever was in the car. I just didn't know if the Jeep could outrun them.

Only one choice. I kept my foot on the gas pedal. Nothing was going to slow me down, not with three little lives on the line. As a former FBI agent, I knew full well I was breaking the law, and likely to get a car chase started. Well, shit, let's take them to the farm and see how they liked facing down a dragon.

"You aren't going to slow down, are you?" Levi asked.

"No. I'm not," I answered. As a father, there was really no decision to be made—I would go to hell and back to do what I had to, break every law on the books, and some not, to make sure I accomplished what I set out to do.

I tightened my hands on the wheel and steered around the traffic in front of me, ducking and dodging between cars, losing the lights behind me for a moment only to see them again a little closer than before.

"They're gaining on us," Levi said, still twisted in his seat. As if I couldn't see that for myself with each look in the mirrors.

"Fuck off!" I yelled, a piece of rage breaking through what little calm control I had left.

Levi flinched, cringing away from me. I shook my head. "Not you, kid, them." But the damage had been done. The hitch in his breathing, the way he held himself tightly, like he was ready and braced for a blow.

If there was nothing else the wolf in me understood, it was pack, family, and loyalty. "Kid, I am not going to hit you. Whether you like it or not, you are part of our family now. That means my job is to protect you the same as I would protect Rylee or Marcella. Understand?"

Slowly he nodded, and while he relaxed a little bit, he was far from easy in his seat.

The wolf I carried was as strong as ever. The Guardian I'd been stayed with me through shifting bodies and losing Faris and his vampire essence that powered his body for hundreds of years.

I wasn't sure I'd ever understand it, and as Rylee had pointed out, it didn't matter. I was still a Guardian, and Faris was gone. Mostly, anyway.

There was one small problem I hadn't shared with Rylee, though—not while she was struggling with her own demons. The last thing she needed was to worry about me.

The thing was, I couldn't shift into my wolf form since Faris and I had parted ways and I'd been left in his body as sole owner. No point in freaking her out when it wasn't necessary, that's what I'd told myself. Maybe I just needed time. But going into this hunt, I could have used that extra bit of ammo in my back pocket.

Another time I'd mull it over. Right now, there was only one task at hand. Get to Seattle as fast as supernaturally possible, and no beat cop would make me slow down because he hadn't met his ticket quota for the day.

The cop car behind me was catching up, even with my foot jammed to the floor on the pedal. I wasn't pulling over; no way. I kept traffic between us, driving so I was alongside a big rig, blocking the cop from actually gaining ground. There was always a way to keep them behind you if you were willing to push the limits.

"Liam . . ."

"Shut it, kid."

The lights were right behind me, the siren now wailing . . . and then the cop pulled onto the shoulder of the highway, using my trick to move up the left side of me.

"Shit balls." I kept the words under my breath, acutely aware of Levi beside me and the way he cringed even when the words weren't directed at him. Rylee, what had you sent with me as a helper? A frightened rabbit whose heart was liable to give out at the critical moment.

I tightened my hands on the wheel, ready to swerve to the left and body slam the other car.

But the cop didn't try to cut me off. He shot past us in a flash of lights. I looked out my side window and for just a moment my eyes and the officer's connected, and I stared hard, taking it all in with a single glance.

The cop was pale, his eyes wide with fear written on every jagged angle of his face, down to the set of his shoulders and the white-knuckled grip he had on the wheel. And there was only one thing to do.

I waited for him to pass and then put the pedal to the floor once more. I tucked the Jeep behind him.

"What are you doing?"

"While I doubt he means to, he's clearing the road for us, and we're letting him be our chaser as far as we can," I said.

"Why didn't he pull us over?" Levi asked, and I wanted to curse Rylee for sending him with me. What was it with teenagers and the constant litany of questions? Pamela was the same way, but at least she came with an arsenal all her own.

Levi came with one thing, and one thing only. A cell phone.

His questions, though, allowed me to keep from thinking about other things, like what we'd left behind at the house.

I put the pieces together slowly, before I spoke. "Rylee told me about a fighter jet that came down when she and Eve were looking for your sister. The pilot . . . told her about an assassination attempt. All of it was internal. I suspect this is more of the same. Problems within the government causing a ripple effect."

He frowned, his brows low over his eyes. "What do you mean, internal?"

I had to work at not snapping at him to shut up and just let me drive. At the same time, he deserved to know what was going on, seeing as this didn't just affect one set of the population. And the distraction really was more welcome than I wanted to let on. It kept me from worrying about what we were leaving behind.

"Someone tried to assassinate the president and it was an inside job. The government is imploding as we speak. The structure of even local governments will start to collapse under the pressure, and the people who are supposed to hold it together, like that cop, are going to be put into situations they aren't really prepared for."

"Holy shit. But wouldn't the news say something about an assassination attempt? Are you sure that really even happened? What wouldn't the cop be prepared for?" Levi turned in his seat so he faced me, his eyes wide.

"No, the media wouldn't necessarily have access to that information. Or they may be muzzled. I'm guessing the government will pull the old bait and switch. They'll show the nation something in the left hand, say a scandal of some sort, while the right hand is getting away with murder. And yes, I am sure." I paused for a moment, thinking my words through, filtering them before I spoke. "As for that cop, I suspect he was being called in on something big. Something that scared him. That's why no sirens."

The thing was, even over the rumble of the tires on the highway, I could hear the scream of jet engines flying high above us. Passing overhead, one after another, and all in the same direction that the cop was headed. Something big for sure, and probably something that made the cop want to shit his pants.

After Rylee told me about the interaction with the pilot, I'd called on my few remaining contacts in the FBI. They'd confirmed things were going to hell in a handbasket made of glass and chicken wire. They saw the end of the world as we knew it coming, and there wasn't anything they could do about it. The current leader of the free world had pissed off enough other nations that they were gunning for him en masse. And the vice president was backing the outsiders in the hopes of keeping his own head attached to his shoulders. I shook my head. It was a clusterfuck, that much was sure.

But I had my own problems to focus on.

Our exit came up, and I took it at high speed, the Jeep bouncing once over a barely there bump. The cop continued on down the highway, his lights still flickering in the fading light of the day.

Down and to the right, we were on a less traveled road littered with potholes. I swerved, knowing where they were before they even came up. Many of the farms in the area had gone under, unable to sustain things with the downturn in the markets, which led not only to the sparse traffic but the shitty road maintenance.

"Is the world going to war?" Levi asked softly, fear lacing his words. "That's what you're kind of saying, isn't it?"

I shrugged as if it wasn't important. "Doesn't matter to me, right now. One task, Levi. One task at a time. Seattle. Female ogre. Back to Bismarck. Understand? We can worry about the world another time."

He nodded slowly. "Okay. One at a time."

The fear wasn't completely gone from him, but it eased a little, at least from what I could tell.

I cranked the wheel and drifted through the final corner that took us down the lane to the farm. Hitting the bumps hard, I was reminded of my first trip to the badlands with Rylee.

Harpies following us, Rylee driving with a small smile on her lush lips, Alex screaming in the back about bumps. The unicorn crush as they'd come into view and the way my heart had pounded with a recognition, that at the time, I'd denied.

This was my world, it always had been. It was partly why I'd not been able to leave Rylee alone, even after she'd been cleared of her sister's death. The other reason was, of course, that she was my mate, even then. Neither of us had been ready, though; we'd needed time. I snorted to myself and hit the brakes.

Levi made a move to get out and I grabbed his arm, stopping him. "No, wait in here."

"Why?"

"Because Eve just had a baby and she doesn't know you."

"Eve?"

"A Harpy. And you don't want a freaked out Harpy coming for you." I got out of the Jeep and started toward the barn.

The structure was still standing—barely, but it provided some cover and a nest for what we believed were the final two, and now three, Harpies in the world. "Eve?"

A screech filled the air and Eve hopped out of the barn through an opening in the side, a tiny fluff ball following her. Literally, the baby Harpy was like a giant buff-colored cotton ball on two dark brown sticks for legs. But the eyes on the cotton ball, they would have given it away if nothing else. Great big golden eyes stared out at me from within the depths of the fluff. I struggled not to grin. The image was that of a creature that couldn't hurt a fly, never mind become one of the deadliest predators in the supernatural world.

Eve blinked several times as she drew close, tipping her head to one side. "Liam, what are you doing here?"

I looked over my shoulder and beckoned to Levi to get out. He did as I asked, staring at Eve and the baby, his jaw hanging open. He kept his back against the vehicle and his hand on the door. Good self-preservation instincts in him at least.

"The ogre babies are . . . sick." I refused to say they were dying. "I need to get to Seattle."

She gasped and I went on. "I know you can't leave. So I need to borrow Ophelia. Is she here?"

"She's gone on a fly-about. She should be back soon." Eve flicked a wing and the tip of one feather in my direction. "Watch the babies. I'll go get her."

Before I could say a word, she launched into the air. Cotton Ball screeched and hopped after her mother, flapping what I suspected were two bits that would eventually grow into wings, but for the moment, they were just more fluff. Waiting was not something I did well.

I crossed my arms over my chest and tried to think about the growing details of my plan. Seattle was a big city, but Rylee said the ogres were in Kerry Park.

"Kid, look up Kerry Park and the surrounding area on your phone."

"Okay." The relief in his voice was palpable.

I looked up as the baby Harpy, Selene, if I remembered right, turned back my direction. Giving up on her mother, she promptly rushed me.

Harpies were dangerous at the best of times. I wasn't sure this was a good idea in the least, but how was I going to stop the fluff ball?

I held my hands out as she plowed into my arms. A shudder rippled through her as she tried to all but climb up my body, her baby claws digging into the ground as she half hopped in her efforts.

"Easy, Cotton Ball." I patted what I thought was the top of her head but wasn't entirely sure with the way she puffed out. Big googly eyes peered up at me, blinking rapidly with three sets of eyelids. "Your mom will be back soon." How many times had I said that to the five babies when Rylee had been on her last salvage? More than I could count, and with only the hope that indeed she would come home. Not that I thought she'd leave forever, but I didn't know when she'd be able to find herself. A week. A month. A year. Whatever it took to deal with the vampire nature she was so opposed to.

While Rylee struggled, thoughts had floated in my brain, thoughts I knew were not mine. Thoughts I *knew* were leftover remnants of Faris. Like muscle memory, I could still call on his knowledge here and there. And with Rylee, his information had been crystal clear.

Let her go, let her figure it out or someone will get hurt. Someone she loves, and then she would never forgive herself.

To leave had been the hardest thing to tell her, to tell her we would be okay. All of it had been true, but that didn't mean I was really okay with her leaving when she'd been in such an obvious state of distress.

"Wait, did she say babies?" Levi asked, his voice pitching into an octave that could only mean one thing.

"Oh, crap," I muttered. As if in answer, from out of the barn tumbled three dragon fledglings, about twice the size of Eve's cotton ball.

I'd met the terrible trio, and they made the ogre babies look tame and quiet on a wild day. One red, one blue, and one pale purple. Two boys and a girl, and no names that we'd been told, so we'd taken to calling them by color. They were about the size of large ponies, and growing fast. As they spied me, three sets of eyes lit up and one of them squalled my name, or mangled it as the case was.

Leeeem! Friend! Purple yelled, making me clutch at my head with one hand. She raced ahead of the two boys. I scooped Selene out of the way, pushing her away a few feet at the last second as Purple bowled into me. I wobbled and crashed to the ground with a heavy thud. Selene screeched and fluffed herself out as though she were truly irritated, though I knew she was no more afraid of the oversized lizards than I was.

Levi, though, was having his first interaction with dragons, no matter that they were babies and not even looking at him. Until he moved. He scrambled backward, onto the hood of the Jeep. Red strode over and took a swipe at his legs, forcing him onto the roof. "Leave him alone, Red," I said from the ground.

Want to play? Red queried while half climbing the Jeep.

"No," I pointed at the dragon and firmed my voice as much as I could while held to the ground by his sister, "he doesn't want to play. Leave him alone."

Red slumped, his lower lip sticking out so far, he'd trip on it if he wasn't careful. He drooped, his wingtips dusting the ground as he wandered toward me.

With the three dragons standing over me, they each took turns sniffing my clothes. *Leeeem, you smell funny.* Red squinted one eye and ran his tongue over his lips.

"Like what?" I couldn't help but wonder what they were smelling. Maybe the coffee I'd spilled on my pants that morning. Or the smell of all the creatures in the house in Bismarck.

Somebody sick? Blue frowned, and the shape of his face, the curve of the bones around his eyes were all Blaz, another friend lost in the fight to save the world.

I nodded slowly, knowing that while they were children, there would be no hiding the truth from them. That was one problem with the supernatural. Children didn't get to stay innocent very long. There was no way to keep them insulated from the realities of our deadly world.

I lifted a hand to Purple's foreleg holding my shoulder down. "Yeah, the ogre babies are sick."

The three of them gasped and sat back on their haunches like dogs, though Blue limped a little. His egg had been cracked when it was laid and there had been a concern that he wouldn't survive. Slower than the other two, the limp was the only thing that held him back, and even that wasn't exactly slowing him down.

Levi slid down from the roof of the Jeep and I motioned for him to come closer. "They won't hurt you, they just get excited when you first meet them. Like big puppies."

"Big puppies that could eat me," Levi muttered. I bit back the grin. He was right, they could eat him, probably in fewer bites than it would take for him to down a cheeseburger.

Purple slunk toward him, popping her head up at

the last second so she and Levi were eye to eye. He froze and she flicked her tongue out, swiping it up his cheek. "What's she doing?" he whispered.

"Just getting a feel for you. Get ready."

"For what?"

Purple tipped her head and I could feel her push her thoughts toward both Levi and me. *Water magic. He has water magic!*

Levi scrambled back. "I heard a voice. Tell me I'm not going crazy."

"No, it's how dragons talk," I said. Selene shoved herself under my one arm, forcing me to hold her as I stood up. Red lay at my feet and Blue just sat back watching the scene unfold. They were unusually quiet and that made me wonder if something was wrong.

Make it rain, Purple demanded. *I want to swim.*

Levi shook his head. "I can't . . . I don't know how."

Purple frowned. *Yes, you can. You can make water, so make water.*

Now that was interesting. "He hasn't learned yet," I said, taking pity on the kid. He nodded hard.

"Yeah, I haven't learned yet."

Oh. When you learn, I want a swimming hole. She left him standing there. He looked at me and I shrugged. "Just don't come back until you can make her a swimming hole and it will be okay."

"Okay?" He swallowed hard. Then swallowed again and put a hand to his stomach like he was going to be sick. "How long before we can go?"

"Just waiting on our ride," I said, scanning the sky

above us. Come on, Eve, find her fast. The sun was setting, and we were losing light. It was January and far from warm. Flying by dragonback was going to make it colder yet. I noted that Rylee had made sure Levi was well outfitted for the possibility, as if she'd known I would let the kid come.

A sudden shrill ringing spun me around, one hand up in defense before I could even think that I wasn't being attacked. Selene screeched and went running toward the barn as fast as her stick legs could take her, and the three dragons went into a spinning frenzy of chasing one another and their own tails.

Levi didn't notice as he pulled the ringing phone out of his pocket. He hit a button and put it to his ear.

"Hello? Yeah, we're at the farm." He glanced at me. "It's Rylee, I'm putting her on speaker so you can talk to her."

Even knowing how smart she was, I found myself ridiculously pleased that she'd put this together. Finding technology that worked close to Rylee and me was tough. With Levi, I had my own secretary, and Rylee and I had a solid line of communication while I was away. I nodded. "Do it."

I kept my distance, a good twenty feet.

He hit another button. "You're on."

"Liam, Doran is here."

"Good, can he do anything? Tell me he can help them." Tell me that they weren't dying.

She paused and I heard it in the space of her breath, the fear, the tears at the back edge of the words. "Forty-eight hours, Liam. After that, there is no bringing them back. Even if you get here with milk in hand, we won't be able to stop the slide."

My guts clenched, but I kept my voice even. "I'll be back before then."

"I know." She hung up, just like that. I pointed at Levi.

"Don't lose that phone, no matter what happens."

He nodded and tucked it inside his jacket.

Eve's hunting cry lit the air up as suddenly as the ringing of the phone. I turned my attention to the sky. Selene answered her mother, and we all rotated toward the sound of whooshing feathered wings and the heavier thud of Ophelia's far larger, taut leathery scaled wings as they beat at the air.

The huge red dragon swept downward, her body backlit by the setting sun. She was a sight with her glittering ruby-colored scales, forty-foot wingspan, and long graceful neck. At the top of which, her jaws were full of three limp deer. As she drew close to us, she hovered ten feet up. From there, she dropped the three deer and I realized they weren't dead yet. The thud of the fall stunned them, and their legs still kicked here and there.

I looked over to see Levi blanch. "She's teaching them to hunt."

He didn't answer as the triplets raced away from us and launched at the deer, one per fledgling. They snapped the fragile necks in a matter of seconds, ending whatever suffering the beasts had, ending the fear.

Ophelia stepped around her children, hiding the sight of them feeding with the bulk of her body.

Liam, Eve tells me the ogre babies are in dire straits? Ophelia dropped her head so we were eye level. I ignored the sound of Levi stuttering behind me. One day this would be normal for him, and he wouldn't even blink. Until then, though, it was best to pretend I didn't even notice his shock.

I nodded. "I need you to take me to Seattle and be my backup. I know that I am asking you to leave those three monsters, but I can't go on my own. Not when lives are on the line. If it was anything else, I wouldn't ask."

Eve fluffed herself up as she drew closer, Selene once more glued to her side. "I will watch them. They like me and they are all strong enough to take on most supernatural creatures on their own. If that is acceptable, Ophelia?"

The red dragon's brow furrowed and she closed her eyes as though a shot of pain ran through her.

How long must we be away?

"Two days at most. If we leave now, maybe less." I knew what I asked of her, to leave her children after losing Blaz . . . it was going to be hard to convince her.

The silence stretched long enough that I began to wonder if I should repeat myself.

I can take you there. Ophelia said. *But I . . . I must come back right away. I can't stay with you.*

I gritted my teeth, already feeling the loss of her help, but knowing she would have a reason. I knew she would not leave me on my own without just cause;

that wasn't like her at all. "Then let's go, we'll find another way back. Levi, meet Ophelia."

I strode to the Jeep, jerked the back door open and grabbed my bag. I pulled the heavier coat out and slid it on, which left the bag sparse. Only a few weapons really, but it was better than going in empty-handed. I slung the bag over my shoulder and hurried back to Ophelia. "Ready?"

She didn't even look at Levi, as she snaked her head toward me. I jumped and she slid underneath me, then did the same to Levi, though his jump was more of a startled fall. I grabbed him as he rolled across her back and situated him behind me. We hadn't put together a harness for Ophelia yet. Between laying her eggs and protecting her clutch, she hadn't been interested in having much company other than Rylee. And to be fair, we'd thought there was no rush. No need to hurry something that wasn't necessary.

Within two heartbeats, we were launched into the air.

I cannot leave them for more than the time to take you and fly back. It is too dangerous. The ogres are not the only ones who are seeing their children die off in droves.

"What do you mean?" I asked. Behind me, Levi's hand clutched at the back of my jacket. Over the wind, the sound of his teeth chattering filled the air around us. I glanced at him. He wasn't cold, I could see it in his face. He was damn terrified. Of course, he would be afraid of heights. He heaved once and I glared back at him.

"Don't you dare puke."

"I'm sorry."

I shook my head. "Just close your eyes. Breathe through your nose and out your mouth."

He nodded and leaned his head against my back, the shuddering of his breathing taking up a steady rhythm.

We were above the farm, looking down. None of Ophelia's children looked up from their meal. Not even Blue, which I thought he might, seeing as of the three of them he needed his mother's protection the most with his limp.

While they are strong enough on their own, I can't leave them yet. Not yet.

"Well, I can understand that. I wouldn't leave if I didn't have to," I said, not entirely understanding her need to explain the obvious.

She shook her head as she beat the wind with her wings. *No, you don't. Dragons don't stay with their hatchlings for more than a week. Dragons are left on their own within seven days of life outside of their eggs. They are either strong enough to survive, or they are picked off by other creatures.* She paused and a shudder rippled through her. *The dragons that are left after the disease, they are mad with fear. They are actively hunting our own kind, their minds broken with what they believe happened. I have heard rumors they are being rounded up by elementals.*

Well, shit, that put a whole new spin on things. Elementals were not supposed to interfere. The fact that Lark (a bad-ass elemental who'd helped us in the battle against Orion) did so on a regular basis was the reason she was anathema among her own people.

The rest of what the dragon said sank in. Ophelia had been with her three fledglings for over a month, far longer than a single week.

"I don't think you are wrong. Things are changing, Ophelia. You don't have to follow the old rules if they don't work. We can't, not if we're going to survive what's coming."

What do you mean?

I frowned, trying to find the right words, feeling them on the tip of my tongue. "The world feels like it's on the edge of something big again. Like the demons were the tipping point, an opening that's left the world vulnerable to something as dangerous."

A sigh rippled through her. *I don't want my children to be weak, Liam. They are some of the last. It will be a struggle as it is to find them mates. But to think I am protecting them only to have them watch the world around us die . . . that feels wrong. Is there nothing we can do?*

It was my turn to sigh. "I don't know. Nothing right now. Maybe our job is just to hang on and ride the damage out this time."

We soared above the clouds, silence except for Levi's heavy breathing behind me.

Will you tell me what is wrong with the ogre babies?

Her words brought the image of Bam and Rut clinging to one another as though they could somehow save each other. I shut the image down before it could settle in my mind's eye.

"They need an ogre mother's milk to survive. Some species of animals are like that, apparently." I tightened my hold on one of her thick red spines, stabilizing myself as she banked to the left, riding a current of air. Behind me, Levi gripped my coat tighter, leaning into me.

"I think I'm going to be sick."

"Off to the right if you're going to—"

His body lurched and he hung to the right. I waited until the sound of liquid splatting down Ophelia's side and then the subsequent dry heaving subsided before I went on.

"If we don't convince another ogre to come and be their wet nurse, they will die."

And is there a time limit?

I did a quick tally in my head. "Less than forty-eight hours now. They don't have much time left, they are . . . they are wasting away." I clenched my jaw, hating the feeling of not being able to move. I knew that we were moving, but my body, the drive of the wolf in me, wanted actual physical movement to keep the fear and growing anxiety at bay. I bit back the howl that rose up my throat, clearing my throat before I spoke again. "Two days is all I've got."

A rumble rolled through her and she picked up speed, flattening out like an arrow shooting through the sky.

Then we need to give it everything we have, both for their sakes and the sakes of my own children. Her voice was hard as steel, the voice of a mother who knew how to protect her babies no matter the cost. The defiance of death for children who were not her own, but those of who she cared for, was as strong a drive as that to protect her own. Around us the air crackled and thickened with ozone, pressing down on us with a pressure that made my ears pop. I looked up as a whirling band of clouds spun toward us. A sharp wind from behind whipped up and sent the forming cyclone away, driving us hard.

"Ophelia," I said, "tell me that's you."

It's me, wolf. It will take much of my strength but I can pull on the weather to push us.

I only wished she'd given us warning about the lightning.

CHAPTER 2

A BOLT OF BRILLIANT, blue-white lightning flowed out of the sky and danced around us. It forked and split over and over again until there was a web of lightning hovering over our heads.

"Fuck, Ophelia, I'm not sure this is a good idea." I was thinking of Levi more than anything. I was pretty sure I could survive a brush with lightning, but I didn't know how much he could take. How strong was the elemental blood in him, and was it enough to protect him?

It looked like we were about to find out.

"Levi, hang on!"

The web of electric blue lightning loosed as though shot from a weapon. Hissing and crackling, it kissed along Ophelia's wingtips and rushed through me and consequently through the kid. Power like nothing I'd ever felt lit me up, my nerve endings and muscles screaming—not in pain, but sheer energy.

Of course, we weren't grounded, so the lightning had nowhere to go but *in* us. A howl ripped out of my throat at the same time a roar escaped Ophelia and a scream from Levi. Underneath me and the boy, Ophelia's muscles bunched, her wings swept down and back with a stroke that shot us forward as if we'd previously been hovering in air, unmoving.

The wind screamed as we sped through the cold, dark night air.

The sheer velocity began to pull at me, and I was wishing we'd taken the time to get a harness together for her.

I bent at the waist, doing my best to reduce the drag on my body. Carefully I reached back and took one of Levi's hands. "Slide your arm through my belt!"

He fumbled under my jacket, but managed to get one hand around my leather belt.

I clung to her, and Levi to me, as the force of the wind pulled us in every direction. A little warning next time, was all I could think. I didn't dare think about what would happen if we slipped off. Ophelia felt like she was barely able to control the headlong flight as it was, never mind turn the power off and spin around to catch us if we fell.

"Liam, I'm slipping!" Levi yelled.

I reached back with one hand, and grabbed the edge of his jeans. "I've got you, just don't let go."

I could barely open my eyes, the wind was so fierce. I turned my head sideways in an effort to see if I could somehow change position to help Levi get more secure in his seat.

A flash of metal, tailed by a burst of flame, had me staring to our left. A jet screamed toward us. "Ophelia!"

I see it.

She rolled as the jet approached and I was upside down, and Levi was hanging, staring up into my eyes.

I was the only thing holding onto him, the only thing keeping him from falling. The look in his eyes as he hung upside down, it would haunt me. He'd thought I was going to drop him. And had fully accepted that he was going to die.

"I've got you," I said, even while my fingers slipped on the waistband of his jeans.

More incoming. Hang on, you two.

Shit, that was not going to help, not one bit.

Ophelia righted herself, and Levi slammed into the scales beside me. I pulled him up and jammed him in front of me. "Hang onto the scales." I wrapped my arms around him, and dug my hands into the red spines. "This is about to get rough."

"That wasn't rough?" he squeaked.

"Not by a long shot."

"Fuddruckers," Levi whispered.

The rumble of more jet engines snapped my head around. Two more jets raced toward us, though these were not from the same team by the shape of the wings and paint. Ophelia dodged them both with ease, rolling and twisting in the air while never really losing her own speed. I kept a grip on the kid, so hard that I knew he probably was struggling to breathe. But it was that or have him hanging by his underwear again.

I watched the jets disappear, noting the colors and symbols told a very interesting story. Two jets were American. The first had been Canadian. And shots had been fired between the three.

They are fighting again. Even after we saved them? The ingrates.

"The humans, you mean?" I yelled into the wind, not because I wasn't sure. But you never knew with a dragon what they were picking up on in your head. Always best to be crystal clear when someone could read your thoughts like reading the newspaper.

Who else? They are the only fools who can't seem to realize we must all coexist on the same planet. They are the ones who keep creating mass weapons, who hate with a virulence that leaves their children afraid to step outside, and their women afraid to trust any man, and their men stupidly thinking they can change it all with more weapons. Idiots. They're going to end up killing us all, aren't they?

She was right, and I knew it, but I didn't want to agree, not out loud. Almost as if by agreeing, I was somehow making it become a reality I did not want to see.

Hell, I'd been a human a lot longer than I'd been a supernatural. That didn't mean I wouldn't help them. I understood what Rylee had meant when she said she knew something bad was coming, but it wasn't entirely clear, and there wasn't much we could do about it until that clarity came through. However, between her info and what I'd gotten from my contacts, I could put together a pretty good picture.

The world was on the brink of another war. And this one would be with weapons that could wipe out the entire planet if it wasn't stopped. There would be no reason to try to save anyone if we let this happen.

There was an explosion and two of the jets

erupted midair, leaving only a single American jet flying. Shrapnel blasted in every direction, flames shot through the clouds in bright sprays. Ophelia didn't say a word, just climbed higher.

Levi shook in front of me. "I'm freezing, and I can barely breathe."

"Don't think about it," I said. "You aren't human, this won't kill you." I hoped. He was sucking wind hard, but he hadn't passed out. Something he would have done had he been fully human at this height. We were way above the clouds and the air was thin.

Ophelia kept her pace up while she spoke.

They won't stop until their world is dead and their species extinct.

"Maybe that would be for the better." The words slipped out and I shook my head, denying them right away. I knew it was a knee-jerk reaction, but I couldn't help it. We'd saved the world, only to watch it disintegrate into a human-made war? That wasn't going to happen. I prayed.

If we let them fight like that, they could end up taking us with them.

The truth in her words echoed what I'd already been thinking. So I changed the subject.

"How long before we get to Seattle?"

We are almost there, Liam. Where do you want me to take you?

I checked the positioning of the sun. Two hours was all it had taken, faster even than a commercial flight. In front of me, Levi's head was ducked and he clung to Ophelia's spine as though he would be swept off at any moment. Here and there he shivered, but otherwise, he didn't move. I had to give him credit, he hadn't completely lost it, despite almost being dumped from the dragon's back.

Which was saying a lot considering the situation.

I checked myself; it was time to focus. Two hours, and the plan I had was still barely sketched out. It looked like I was about to pull a Rylee and leap before I looked.

From what Rylee said, the majority of the ogres camped out in Kerry Park, but that was a small strip of green according to Levi's phone. The likelihood of it actually being their real haunt was small. But I wasn't about to ask to be dropped in the middle of where their last known whereabouts was. Call it a feeling, but I doubted my sudden appearance and request for one of their females was going to go over well. Of course, it's what Rylee would have done, fully expecting to fight her way out and win. A grin twisted my lips.

"Let's do a fly-over, see if we can see any ogres, or a good place to land." She nodded and banked to the side, heading to the north.

A few minutes passed and we slid over a small section of green. "Can you drop lower?"

Of course.

She spun us downward until we were only about a hundred feet above the treetops. A faint whiff of ogre musk was there and gone in a flash. I might not be able to shift into my wolf form, but my nose worked as well as it ever had, even as a human.

"Levi, try your phone. See if it can tell us where we are."

Shivering, he sat up slowly and fished around in his jacket. "The screen is dark. I don't understand, I had like eighty percent still."

"Supernaturals and technology don't mix," I muttered. "It might come on later when you are away from me and Ophelia."

He looked over the side of her carefully. "That's Kerry Park."

"You sure?"

"Yes, see that building there?" He pointed at a large blocky structure across from the green space, and I nodded.

"Yeah, I see it."

"I remember it when I did the search for the area. That sign on top of it is hard to miss."

The sign in question said something along the lines of the current president was going to cause the apocalypse. Another day, another life, I would have laughed. Not so much now after all I'd seen.

"Good job, kid," I said. I scanned the area, seeing in the distance a glimmer of water. "Head to that lake, Ophelia."

You got it. That will be a good place for me to rest before I head back.

"That little green space back there is hiding ogres?" Levi mumbled, twisting to look behind us. "That's not possible. I mean, is it?" He looked at me, awkward with the fact that I was holding him in front of me.

Ophelia snorted and shook her head. *The world of the supernatural rarely fits into what is possible. The place may look small to you, but with the right magic, they could bend it in on itself and make it a monstrous forest you would never escape from if they chose.*

I startled, surprised. "Seriously?"

She nodded. *Yes. Be wary; if they have a mage that can do that, you will have to truly watch yourselves. As you've seen, ogre mages are even more vicious than the rest of their warriors. Bloodthirsty assholes, the bunch of them, if you ask me. The only good ones are those three you will raise, because I know you will show them a better path.*

There was more than a hint of rage simmering under her words; grief thick and heavy swam over the syllables, making them hard to stomach. Her loss had been as great as any of ours. Blaz had been her mate, the father of her children, and he'd fought her a long time before he let himself realize that truth. And then he'd been killed by a band of ogres.

I put a hand to her side. "I miss him too. We all do."

She bobbed her head. *I know. I only wish it had not ended the way it had. All dragons expect to die, but not at the hands of a creature we could snap in half with a single bite.*

I gritted my teeth as she flew lower to the lake, doing my best to fend off the emotions that flowed from Ophelia into me. By the way Levi trembled, he was getting a dose of it too.

I'd never mentioned it to Rylee, but Ophelia's way of speaking was very different than Blaz's. Blaz was your typical male, straightforward and blunt.

Ophelia's words held emotion like a cup held water, and if you drank from it, those emotions spilled into your own mind. Maybe Rylee didn't notice. Or maybe it was just the difference between male and female.

The emotions eased as she focused on bringing us down. The bobbing turbulence of landing setting my teeth on edge, and my stomach rolled more than once as we bounced along. Levi gasped as we slid through the downward air currents, which shook us sideways hard, before landing on a strip of beach tucked in a tiny cove. Ophelia's claws dug into the soft dirt, back feet and tail dipping into the water with barely a splash.

I unwrapped my arms from the kid and jumped from Ophelia's broad back, sliding down the left side, away from where Levi had emptied his stomach. Levi was right behind me, stumbling on wobbly legs as he hit the ground.

She turned her head to us, big eyes blinking. She flicked her tongue out once. *I will wait as long as I can. I will need an hour at least to rest before I can head home.*

I put a hand on her side. "Thank you. Hopefully we can make this happen fast." I said the words but I think we both knew there was no way I was going to find a female ogre, convince her to come with me, and do it in an hour. Without causing any other problems along the way, at least.

Even my luck was not that good.

She bobbed her head, eyes clouded with concern. *Rylee would not be happy if I left her mate, without even trying to wait for him. If nothing else, I will do a sweep of the city for you before I leave.*

I laughed, then realized she was serious. "You have no faith in me?"

As we flew I recalled that I have heard of this ogre tribe, but I assumed they would have gone in with the rest who were killed. They are . . . violent is too mild of a word. They are masochistic in the way they treat one another, and they treat outsider supernaturals as chattel and food. They are incredibly dangerous, Liam.

"Great," I grumbled. "Anything else?"

She squinted her eyes in thought. *They are stronger and faster than the rest of the ogres out there, which is partly why they cut themselves off from the rest of their species. They are the ultimate killers.*

I'd faced ogres before. Most were over seven feet in height and had a musculature that would rival the biggest body builders. They were fast, and they loved nothing more than a good fight.

So if this tribe was even more dangerous . . . as Rylee would say . . . fuck me. I drew in a breath. "Numbers?"

Many, many. I don't know exactly, I only heard about them from those who'd passed by. But they are a big tribe from all accounts. A big mob. And if they have a mage . . . that will make your task multiply in difficulty like rabbits in the spring.

I scrubbed a hand over the back of my neck. We were into midnight hours with maybe six more before dawn broke, and every minute that ticked by was against me. This was no time for a long goodbye.

"Thank you, Ophelia. For everything."

She winked one big eye and laid her head on the sand. *Be careful.*

"We will." At least as much as we were able to in the situation.

I sniffed the air, the smell of a multitude of animals, most not natural to the area, coursing back to me. I frowned as I plucked through the different scents. Too many animals in one place: my first thought was that it could be a holding pen for the ogres' next meals.

"Come on, Levi. This way," I said.

He shivered beside me in the dark, his eyes downcast.

Ophelia lifted her head a few feet. *One last thing. Don't die. I don't want to be the one to take that news to Rylee. She would never forgive me for letting you die.*

I grimaced, wondering for a moment if Ophelia felt like that toward Rylee. Like she would never really forgive her because Rylee had been with Blaz when he died. He'd been protecting her, as was his job, but he'd left behind Ophelia and unborn children. I wisely kept my thoughts to myself, though.

Levi flinched as if she'd smacked him.

"She doesn't mean that, does she?" he asked, his eyes barely lifting to mine.

I shrugged. "Death is something we deal with all the time."

He frowned. "No, I mean would Rylee really not forgive her?"

I glanced at him as I walked up the beach to the tree line. "Rylee would forgive her. She has a heart that can't hold a grudge." But I knew what he was really worried about was if I died while with Levi, would Rylee let him come back. Levi and his sister had only been with us a few days, but I had no doubt it was the first time in their short lives they'd been safe and able to sleep at night without waiting for their door to bust open. His face was an open book: he didn't want to lose that safe place if I didn't make it through the ogres we were going to have to face.

"Don't worry about Rylee. If anything happens she won't blame you, kid."

Faris was proof enough of Rylee's ability to see all sides of the story.

I could almost feel the vampire laughing softly and I frowned. He was gone, his soul having crossed the Veil to the other side when the sunlight burnt him out of his body.

But . . . now and again, I could still feel Faris, almost like a ghost only I could sense. It was another thing I wasn't prepared to talk to Rylee about. At least not yet. I wasn't sure if it was his memories coming through the synapses of a brain we'd shared, or my imagination.

Not your imagination, you know that, he whispered as if he stood beside me.

I hurried through the trees, picking my way easily in the dark, ignoring his voice. My eyes adjusted, but of course—behind me Levi crashed to the ground.

"Sorry. I can't see," he mumbled.

I turned, adjusted the bag on my shoulder, and opened it. At the bottom was a small flashlight.

I pulled it out, flicked it on, and pointed it at the ground. "Keep it away from my eyes and yours."

He took it with a nod. With him and the light behind me, the way ahead was clearer yet.

We moved—well, not silently—but quickly through the trees. I had to give Levi credit, he didn't complain, not even when I heard him stub his toes, or stumble into a hole he didn't notice. He just got back up and hurried to catch up. We cut across the green space, heading west toward the scent of animals that called to the wolf in me. What the hell were those fucking ogres up to?

I paused as the trees thinned and drew in a deep breath.

My wolf stretched forward, identifying everything I picked up on. Every kind of mammal, birds, reptiles, the numbers were staggering. I shook my head. That wasn't possible. I had to be getting something wrong. I hurried forward, drawn by a curiosity that detoured me from the reason we were there.

Or perhaps the wolf in me knew something I didn't. I was betting on my wolf. He was a tough bastard.

A large fence grew out of the forest, wrought iron, twelve feet high, razor wire at the top. I stared at it, thinking. Was it possible that the ogres had a second compound within this green space and we'd stumbled on it?

No, even my luck wasn't that good. Logic kicked in and I knew exactly what we were looking at, and it wasn't an ogre compound.

"That looks . . . bad," Levi said. I reached back, grabbed him around the waist by his jeans and threw him up and over the fence. He screeched in mid-air and an answering screech from a nearby aviary burst through the night like a series of gun shots.

"Shut up," I snapped as I climbed up the fence, pausing at the razor wire. I swung my bag first, covering the worst of the wire. Hanging by my hands, I swung my legs up and over, landing on top of my bag. From there, I leapt down on the inside of the fence line and landed inside the enclosure.

I climbed back up the wrought iron and pulled my bag down. There was no guarantee we were coming out the way we came in.

"Seriously, a little warning would have been nice, dude," Levi muttered, brushing himself off.

I shrugged. "We're in a hurry, I didn't need a vote to tell me what I was going to do."

The signage as we hurried along the path stopped him in his tracks. "If we're in a hurry, then why are we going through a zoo?" he asked, not a drop of heat in his voice. Very unlike the other teenagers I knew. Then again, he'd had the shit beaten out of him regularly by his father. That didn't leave much room for defiance in any soul.

I didn't have an answer for him, not really. Why the hell *was* my wolf taking me through a damn zoo? I didn't have a clue, but it felt right. Almost as if someone called to me.

"Turn the flashlight off," I said.

He did as I asked, again without question.

I let the deeply rooted instinct in me take the lead. I followed my nose past enclosures of various kinds, some heavy with bars, others barely chicken wire, depending on the type of animal behind them. I barely saw the animals, though I could have named them by their scents. Zebra, chimpanzee, peacock, bear, and cougar. We passed the giraffes, and they blinked at us from well above our heads, their eyes following us.

Levi kept close. "What are we doing here?"

I answered him truthfully. "I don't know."

"Great."

I wasn't bothered that we were in the zoo, other than the time it was taking away from my search. But I'd learned with Rylee that there was a reason things happened, and while we were on a time crunch, *something* had brought us this way. The why of it was yet to be answered, but whatever it was calling to me hadn't let up yet. I felt it like a pull through my soul, and my wolf wasn't about to be denied. The tension grew, like elastic being pulled taut, ready to snap at any second.

I didn't have to wait long to see where we were being led.

We followed the curving paved path around a sloping corner and came face to face with a large cat enclosure. There were wide flat stones in the middle of it, sand, a few scrub bushes, all made up to look like an African savannah. A slow rolling man-made river flowed around the edge of the structure, and I wondered if there was a crocodile or two floating about. For authenticity, of course.

I drew in a deep breath, tasting for the first time

a scent that was all fire, as if the sun suddenly had a scent all its own.

Lions.

My wolf all but nodded. I approached the enclosure, taking it in. There was a small fence hip height to keep the public at a reasonable distance. A green space of maybe ten feet, and then there was a second, taller fence easily fifteen feet high of solid steel mesh. Beyond that was the actual enclosure itself with a third fence even higher and the makeshift moat six feet across.

It seemed overkill to me, and I wondered about the lions, why the enclosure would be set up this way.

I slipped off my coat and handed it and the bag of weapons to Levi. "Don't lose this. If someone comes, hide."

He raised an eyebrow as he took the bag, a flash of personality finally coming through the abuse. "This seems a bad time to commune with nature, if you ask me."

My lips twitched. "Thanks, I'll take it into consideration."

Although, I asked myself the same question. What the hell was I doing? I was here in Seattle and my first task was to find a female ogre, not go to the zoo to check out the lions.

But that pull was still there, and my wolf all but shoved me forward. Whatever was going on, I needed to get in that lions' pen.

Stupid, a part of my head warned me. Very stupid.

I ignored it, and hopped over the first fence. I

strode across the green space, noting there were tiny depressions in the ground. Sensors of some sort? I bent and brushed a finger over one. It was a sensor with a red light that went out when I touched it. So I could short-circuit whatever it was. Was that good or not?

I stood and headed to the second fence. The steel mesh was an easy climb, but I took note of certain things that made me think perhaps my wolf didn't know as much as he thought he did.

Like the thin wiring that wrapped around the mesh that looked suspiciously like electric shock wires.

A cold sweat broke out along my spine as I climbed. The electricity could come on at any second, and while there was a chance I would short circuit it just being supernatural, there was a chance the current was strong enough it could still work on me. Which brought the scene from *Jurassic Park*, where the kid gets blasted off the fence, to mind rather suddenly.

I hurried my climb.

At the top, I swung a leg over and dropped on the other side into a crouch. I held still, feeling the air thicken, not unlike the ozone in the clouds right before the lightning struck. I scented the air, drawing it over the back of my tongue. A low growl rumbled out of my chest without warning.

The heavy sun-filled, hot incense that was unique-ly lion filled the air, growing stronger with each passing second.

The heavy thud of padded feet approaching kept me where I was in a crouch. From the back of the lion enclosure emerged a male easily twice the size of any normal African lion. His mane was black, his body a brilliant gold that glimmered even in the dark of night, and his eyes . . . his eyes were silver.

He was a Guardian.

CHAPTER 3

"WHAT THE HELL is a Guardian doing in a zoo?" I stood as I spoke. The Guardian continued to approach me, a low rumble in his chest that sounded a bit like a laugh. He sat on his haunches at the edge of the false river, his paws sinking into the soft, wet ground. There was only the one fence between us. And suddenly I was thinking that it had been a bad idea to come over even one fence.

"Well, I could ask you what exactly you are doing here, Wolf." The lion's silver eyes narrowed. "And what happened to you? Your eyes are blue instead of silver."

I shook my head. "Long story. And you are avoiding my question. What are you doing stuck in a zoo? Unless you are here of your own free will? And if you are, why did you call for me?"

He snorted and shook his head, mane flipping about. "No, hardly. I was knocked out, captured, and then sold into this place. As to why I would call on you, take a guess, mutt."

I wasn't buying his story. Something about it wasn't quite right. "Why?"

"Why would I want out?" His voice had a perpetual edge of laughter, like every word was hanging onto humor like a monkey from a branch.

I put my hands on my hips. "That much is obvious, idiot,

but why were you taken? What would be the point of capturing a Guardian?"

He lifted one big paw to me in supplication, pad upward. "Because with the Guardians out of the world, our places, our sanctuaries can be taken. Unlike you, the rest of us are set to guard certain . . . things. You are the wanderer. You are the one who is set to guard the world." He swiped the paw across the dirt in front of him. His eyes were intense, but I didn't look away.

Bits and pieces of what he said were truth. I just didn't know how much. I took a step toward the fence between us. "Then I need to get you out of here if that's the case. You need to get back to taking care of whatever it is you left behind."

"No." He put a paw over his face, as though he couldn't stand the sight of me. "If you try, they will capture you too. No, you must leave this place. Guard your home territory. That is your job, Wolf. Leave me here . . . to rot."

I rolled my eyes. "You don't need to convince me to help you with some attempt at reverse psychology."

He peeked through the toes of his paw. "Really? The last Guardian I drew in just laughed at me."

I lifted an eyebrow. There weren't many Guardians left that I knew of, and the ones I did recall were less than kind. "Wasn't Spider, was it?"

He winked. "That would be the one. She's a real bitch."

"Recently?" I had to still the urge to look over my shoulder. Spider was not to be trifled with.

He shook his head. "No, about six months ago. She was looking for someone who'd taken her by surprise."

Shit, that would be Rylee again. I kept my face still. "Well, let's get you out of here."

I took a look at the final fence. It was steel vertical bars with spaces that would maybe allow me to stuff an arm through. I stared up at the top. As I tried to figure out how to get him out, I continued to interrogate him. "Was it the ogres who captured you?"

"They . . . helped. They had a mage, she is powerful and dangerous. She bound me into this form within the confines of the cage once she realized what I was." His eyes narrowed. "If you're going to do something, get on it, Wolf."

I put a hand on the steel bars, feeling the steady hum of magic within the metal. Magic I'd felt before . . . in the collar I'd worn when I'd been captive to Milly. "This cage keeps you from shifting?"

He nodded. "From what I can tell. I could climb out as a man, but not as a lion."

I gripped the steel harder, thinking to pull it out.

"Stop. You cannot save me. I am resigned to this place. And I do not want to owe my life to a stupid dog. Why the world would make a Wolf the Guardian of us all is beyond me." He snarled, the laughter suddenly gone from his voice. There was more truth in those words than all his previous ones combined.

He wanted to be freed, but he didn't want to owe anyone anything. He didn't want to be beholden to another Guardian, but another Guardian was probably the only one who could free him.

Quite the quandary.

I stepped back, finally understanding why my wolf had brought me to a lion who didn't want freedom bad enough to fight for it. My feet froze. "Maybe you can help me, we can strike a deal. You help me, and I'll help you free yourself."

His ears perked up, the tips flicking back and forth. "How?"

"I cannot . . . shift any longer."

He closed his eyes and a long pink tongue flicked out, smoothing out his whiskers. "A problem some Guardians face when they are too long in one shape or another. You know that already, though, don't you?"

I nodded. "That's not the case, though. I've been trapped in my wolf form and found my way back to my human shape."

His eyes narrowed. "Then it is a matter of need, of desire for the form of the wolf. If you have been stuck like this before, then you know it must be a powerful draw that pulls you through to the other side." He shrugged and I understood two things. One, we were more alike than probably he wanted to believe, seeing as he told me exactly what his own problem was. And two, if he really wanted to shift, even within the cage he could.

There was one thing I knew about alpha males: Their pride didn't take being poked well.

Time to smack the kitty with a stick and see what happened.

"You're afraid to leave, Lion. That is why Spider left you." I laughed as I backed away from him, seeing a fork in the future if I chose it. Helping Lion could change the trajectory of my own quest.

I chose to help him, even though it was going to piss him the fuck off.

He roared at me. "I am not afraid."

I shrugged. "I see a tiny little kitten shivering in his boxed yard. You could shift if you really wanted to." I kept backing away until the fence touched my spine. I held the smile on my lips.

He snarled and lunged at the fence between us. He landed half in the water, his back end sinking as his claws clattered against the steel bars, almost as if he made to climb. "You don't scare me," I said. "You're the ultimate cowardly lion. Enjoy your humans pampering you, pointing at you for the rest of your miserable life."

His snarls ripped through the night as he slid in the moat, his body jerking as he fought to climb upward. "I will kill you, Wolf!"

"I doubt it, seeing as you are too afraid to even bother trying to live. You'd have to shift, and it's obvious you can't even do that." It didn't matter that I couldn't shift, he'd forgotten about that in his rage.

He snarled and roared, splashing through the moat as he fought to reach through to me. His claws swiped uselessly through the air and I just shook my head. I couldn't save him. He had to get himself out of that cage, for I was surely not climbing in to lift him out.

He backed out of the moat, shaking his mane and roaring at me.

I flipped him off, knowing that what I said next would either spur him forward or make him fail. "Weak as a newborn pussy cat. Sad, really, but your territory is probably better off without your supposed Guardianship. Maybe I'll take them a tabby cat to replace you."

I stood with my back against the mesh wire fence with the electrical lines in it. There was a slight humming coming from down the fence. Shit.

His silver eyes all but shot hatred at me. He ran at the fence and launched upward, shifting in mid-air. His body was long and lean, his skin blending into the night as his hands wrapped around the steel bars. He shimmied up and over the fence.

He pointed a finger at me. "You're going to die."

He leapt from the top, shifting once more as he fell. His body hit the ground in front of me, tail twitching, mouth open in a snarl. He crouched, prepped to spring at me.

I saluted him, a grin on my lips. "You're welcome."

I jumped up and sideways, fingers and feet digging into the fence as the electricity began to bounce and hum along the lines. I just needed to get up and over the top and then I could get shocked to hell and it wouldn't matter.

At the top of the mesh fence, the electricity came on. The voltage was as powerful as I feared, and it slammed me between the legs, through my balls and into my belly. The world blanked out, an instant re-start. I fell, thank the gods, to the side Levi was on, though I wouldn't have cared either way.

The ground was soft like a cloud compared to the pain that rocketed through my belly and family jewels. I lay there, twitching, a small part of me wishing that Lion would indeed kill me and stop the pain that sliced me. There was the sound of tearing, the shrieking of metal, and I struggled to place it. Or maybe that was just my body as it still hummed with the shock.

Levi bent over me, his eyes darting to me and then above my head. "Liam, get up, he's clawing his way through the fence."

I rolled to my belly and looked behind me. Lion was indeed tearing through the fence, his claws taking huge chunks out with each swipe. He twitched as the electricity hit him, but it didn't slow him much. The rage in him had not abated. Shit, I'd thought once he realized why I'd pushed his buttons he'd settle down. Apparently not.

I pushed to my feet, staggered and then grabbed Levi's arm. "Okay, time to go."

Levi ran beside me, but he kept looking back. "That lion was . . . talking! Is that normal?"

"I know. Yes, it's normal. Now run if you don't want to be stuffed with catnip and be turned into a kitty toy."

Behind us, there was a particularly loud crack of metal, then the sound of a gun going off. I spun around in time to see Lion leap through the green space between the two fences. Within the ground, those little devices shot upward. Two of them spit out a wire netting, and two others shot out feathered darts. They had to have been tripped by his weight. It was a good thing then that I couldn't shift or my wolf and I would have been tangled up.

Lion dodged them both with ease, saw us and leapt in our direction. Holy damn shit balls.

I pushed Levi ahead of me. "Go, go!"

The sound of the Guardian chasing us down was heavy in my ears, the thud of his pads on the pavement was loud to me. We wove through the zoo, and I kept us a few feet ahead of the Lion, but barely . . . and then he suddenly stopped. The sounds of pursuit gone from one second to the next.

I spun around, expecting anything but what I saw.

The same tall, lean man with jet black hair and dark mocha skin who'd climbed the first fence stared at me. "You . . . you bastard."

I grinned at him, but still kept Levi behind me. "As I said, you're welcome."

His lips twisted up in a perfect imitation of a cat grimace. "Go on, Wolf. This city is not for anyone but the ogres now. And you have given me the . . . encouragement I needed to free myself. For that I will give you this advice." He took a step back, his silver eyes glittering in the night. "This is the city of death. Whatever you seek here, let it go. It isn't worth it. The ogres will come when they realize I am free, and they will find your scent and they will hunt you down. Leave while you still can."

With that he spun on his heel and was gone in a flash of skin and teeth.

I turned and headed toward fence line closest to us.

"Not again," Levi muttered. I grabbed him and launched him over, using my bag again to cover the razor wire for my passing.

The moon was setting, and I felt time passing. Already, I put the Lion behind us, both in thoughts and deeds. His advice was probably warranted, but there was no way I was leaving without a female ogre.

I hurried Levi along, all but herding him through the trees toward the not-so-distant sound of traffic. There was a highway around here, there had to be. Another half an hour slipped by before we emerged onto what did look like a main highway. "Can you see a sign or anything? Are we almost there?" Levi asked, and I stared at him.

"Why, you got somewhere you want to be?"

His shoulders dropped. "I just figured it helps to find where we need to go, if we know where we are first."

I slapped a hand on his shoulder; he flinched, and I eased off. "You're right. And the sign says 99."

He pulled out his phone and brought up the Internet. I leaned over to look and the screen fuzzed up. I backed off. He tick-tacked a few things in, his fingers flying over the miniscule digital keyboard. A part of me was glad I didn't have to deal with technology anymore. My fingers were not meant for detail work. I glanced at my hands and cringed. Strike that, my hands weren't meant for the detail work, but Faris's hands could have worked one of those new phones over, no problem.

"We're about an hour walk from Kerry Park. I mean," he glanced up at me, "if that's where you want to go still?"

I wasn't sure I did. What were the chances there was a female ogre just waiting out in the park for me? Slim to none, and even I knew that.

I rubbed a hand over my face, thinking. Dox was the only ogre I really had ever known and he'd been an outcast from his own kind. He'd run a pub, but had loved to cook; in particular, he had a thing for sweets. I thought about the brownies he made, and how Alex had gone gaga over them. To be fair, anyone who ate Dox's baking had gone gaga over it. Did all ogres like sweets?

This was the only potential clue I had, which meant we were running with it.

"Find a bakery close to Kerry Park." I motioned at Levi.

"A bakery?"

I nodded, waiting while he looked up bakeries in the area on his phone. "There's one about an hour that way, and it's got lots of good reviews," he pointed east, "*and* it will be open in two hours so we wouldn't have long to wait."

I was already walking along the highway. "Then that's the bakery we go to." Fuck, this was a long shot, a toss in the dark that probably wouldn't pan out. But I had no other choice, no other clue. Because rushing over to Kerry Park and asking if I could borrow a female ogre would be like some missionary asking to come in to a gun-toting drunk's house to discuss their salvation through Jesus. In other words, it was a very, very bad idea.

We had two hours before the bakery would open, so there was no point in rushing. At least that's what I told myself even while the wolf in me paced.

We walked in silence for all of two minutes.

"How did you know the lion wouldn't kill us? Or that it wasn't a real lion?" Levi asked. "I mean, there wasn't anything really different about how he looked, was there? Can all animals talk?"

I wondered if Rylee had ever been this irritated with me when I'd started asking questions about the supernatural world. Who was I kidding? I'd irritated her from the first question right through until I stopped. I smiled and did my best to fill Levi in. This was his world too, at least for now. "Not all animals can talk. Guardians like Lion and me are different than other animals. And I didn't know that he wouldn't kill us. I took a calculated chance."

"Then why would you let him out?"

"Because he does have a job for this world. All the Guardians do, even those who are assholes."

He rubbed his hands over his arms as we walked and I could almost see the wheels in his head turning as he processed the new information. "You know when Ophelia ran the lightning over us?"

"Yeah, kind of hard to forget."

"I think . . . I think she woke something up in me."

Now *that* slowed my feet. "What do you mean?"

He held out his hand, palm up, and a small, clear pool of water appeared in the center. The water continued to fill until it spilled off the edges of his hands.

I nodded, not bothered by what he could do. A puddle of water in the hand was hardly helpful in the scheme of things. But no doubt, it would freak the kid out. "Rylee said you were a water elemental, or at least that was the blood running through your veins."

He shook his head. "It doesn't make sense, though. I thought . . . I thought there wasn't enough of that blood to do anything to me."

I shrugged. "It probably does make sense. I just don't know how to explain it. We need someone who actually understands how the bloodlines work to spell things out. Be sure to ask that Jackal when we get back. He can explain most of that stuff since it's his world." I hoped, anyway. Nigel was one of the new additions Rylee met on her salvage for Levi's little sister. While Rylee trusted him . . . he was another canine, and my wolf didn't fully think it was a good idea to let him get too close.

Blessedly, Levi was quiet the rest of the walk to the bakery. I kept an eye on the drifting moon as it dropped lower in the sky, slowly setting. Time passing. I did a quick tally in my head. Forty-one hours and change remaining. We still had lots of time. In theory, of course.

A sudden rush of scents lit up my brain, and I slowed my feet. Something sweet, like an overused perfume, raw milk and . . . ogre. That musk was undeniable, there was nothing out there quite like it.

I put a hand on Levi, pushing him behind me. Could I be that lucky as to find an ogre female outside of the park, away from her apparently psychotic tribe?

Only one way to find out. I kept our pace sedate as I slowly tracked the scent of the ogre. I couldn't tell if it was a female or not, but when we rounded the corner I saw her. She was taller than me but only by a few inches, so that would put her at about six and a half feet.

I shook my head, no more than that. I had to get used to being in a slightly shorter body.

Her skin was a glossy, pure black that I could see glistened even in the moonlight. Here and there were patches of purple, though, like she'd gone through a shower of splatter paint. Her shoulders were hunched under a light top that left her arms and shoulders bare, odd for the cooler weather, and showing a few pale scars. She moved slowly, not seeming to even notice us. A soft sob rippled out of her, and she covered her mouth with one hand, while she wrapped the other around her waist. A sobbing female ogre with scars all over her back and shoulders.

Something was wrong, and every instinct I had screamed at me to watch my back. Ogres were not known for being overly emotional in regards to the softer side of things. Anger, yes, that was a given. Not sobbing, not tears, not oblivious to the world around them. Their sense of smell wasn't on par with mine. But she should have noticed us. We were upwind of her, our scents should have been jammed up her nose already.

I glanced back at Levi, pointed and then put a finger to my lips. His eyes popped open wide and he gave me a slow nod. I began to wonder if his eyes would fall out if they opened wide like that again, like a perpetual jack in the box. But with eyes.

According to the bright screen of Levi's phone, the bakery was just a few minutes away. Apparently the assumption that ogres liked their sweets wasn't so far off base. I motioned for him to put the phone away. I kept us far enough back, shifting so that we weren't upwind of her anymore. At least that would give us a chance that she wouldn't pick up on our scents. Though in the obvious state of distress she was in, I doubted she would notice.

Ten minutes later she reached a park bench and slid into it, her back to us still. She bent at the waist, rocking slowly.

Was she unstable? Shit, that was the last thing I needed. A female ogre who was out of her mind? Was that even possible? I didn't want to think about it too much. Right now, we needed to make contact.

I put a hand on Levi and tugged him back the way we'd come until we could barely see her sitting on the bench.

My mind raced as I formulated a simple plan, something I'd implemented more than once in my FBI days. I bent my head so I could whisper to Levi.

"I want you to walk by her, and when you see her ask her where the bakery is."

"Why?" he whispered back.

"Because I told you to." I tightened my hold on his shoulder, and he trembled under it. I eased off. I really had to remember he wasn't tough like Pamela. Or even Frank. That necromancer had a spine of steel despite being a kid still in his teens.

"No," he shook his head, "I mean why would I be looking for a bakery at . . ." he looked at his phone, "three in the morning?"

That was a good catch. "New job. Bakeries start early."

"But why wouldn't I know where it was?" He frowned. "Your plan stinks."

He shook my hand off and walked away from me, toward where the ogre sat, still crying on the bench. I hissed at him to stop, to come back, but he just hurried his feet, the little shit.

I followed at a slower pace, stopping near a tree about twenty feet away, leaning against it so I could listen.

"Hey, I'm totally turned around and my phone died." He held up his phone, the screen blank. "Do you know the area?"

Her head tipped up, and she swiped a hand over her eyes. "Um. Yeah, I do. Where are you going?"

"I'm supposed to meet a friend near a place called Vanilla and Honey. A bakery, he said." He tucked his phone away in his back pocket.

She twisted on the bench and I ducked behind the

tree, just in case. "You just cross that street over there. It's a couple of blocks down. They'll be doing their early morning muffin and coffee in an hour."

"Thanks, that's what we were going for." There was a pause and I leaned back out to watch the interaction. "Are you okay?" he asked.

She shook her head, and put her hands over her eyes. "No. But . . . you're sweet for asking. Go on now, go see your friend. It's not safe out here at night."

Levi sat on the bench and I stared at him as if I could make him move. Bad idea, very bad idea, don't get close to the ogre who can snap you in half like the kid you are.

"I can't just leave you like this. Do you want me to walk you home?"

She laughed, but it was choked up. "What, you think you can protect me?"

He flushed, and ducked his head. "I guess not."

Time to make my move. I stepped out around the tree, not bothering to hide my approach with softened steps. "He might not . . . but I can."

CHAPTER 4

SHE SPUN AS she stood, her eyes wide, her body shaking so hard, the ends of her hair shook. "Who are you?"

Levi stayed where he was. Maybe he was smarter than I gave him credit for. The last thing I wanted was for him to draw her attention now that she was somewhat pinned between us. I held up both hands, palms forward in the universal sign of no harm. "My name is Liam, and I am a Guardian."

Her chest heaved as she sucked wind hard, as if she had been running flat out. "Even a Guardian can't protect me. And why would you bother? We aren't the same species." She took a step back. "No one can save me."

I kept my approach slow, as if trying to calm a wild animal.

"Save you from what?" Levi asked.

She glanced at him and then back to me. "I'm not telling you anything. You two are outsiders." She spat the last word at me, but it lacked heat.

I shrugged, fighting the urge to just thump her over the head and drag her with me. I needed her to want to come with us. There was no way I could force her hand. "I may be an outsider, but I'm not the one afraid to be here in Seattle. You are."

Her lips trembled. "You *should* be afraid. My tribe will kill you. And him just because he's with you." She motioned at Levi with a tip of her head. He stiffened. I shook my head and forced a smile to my mouth.

"That's not going to happen. We're going to be gone before they even know we're here."

"Then why would you even come? Just to prove you can?" Her tone suggested others may have done the same in the past. Again, I shook my head.

"No, I think I am here to save you from whatever it is that makes you cry. And to ask for your help."

Her mouth made a perfect O and tears slipped from her cheeks. "You think you can give me back my child? More the fool are you."

Her words shot through me so hard, I stood and stared at her as she started away. I almost couldn't get the words out, they stuck in my throat so hard, the disbelief holding them there.

"And if I can give you not one child, but three? Triplets? Ogre babies who need a mother."

She stumbled and spun, hands clenched into fists. "What did you say?"

Time to throw caution to the wind. "Three ogre babies. Triplets that need a mother, an ogre mother. Without you, they are going to die." Time to be bold. I approached her and carefully took both her hands in mine. "Please help me save them. We are running out of time."

Her whole body trembled, as if on the verge of falling to the ground, and her eyes slowly closed. "My tribe. They . . . they're going to kill me. You can't save me from them, they're too strong, and too vicious. I'm . . . I would help you if I could."

"I can get us out of here. If you'll let me." I

motioned for Levi and he moved to my side. "Show her the pictures of the triplets."

He flicked his phone on and pulled up a picture of the babies from the day before. Sleeping, they didn't look sick at all. "They don't have long without your help. The blue boy is Kav, the purple on the left is Rut, and on the right there is Bam." Names, give them names and faces and she'd be hard pressed to say no.

Tears spilled over her cheeks and she hiccuped a soft sob. "They're beautiful."

"And they are dying." I struggled with the words, struggled to impart the emotion that would help her see she was desperately needed. That she hadn't flat out denied us was beyond what I'd truly hoped. I would fully admit to myself that I'd come to Seattle believing I would fail, believing that no matter what I did, it would not be enough.

"Please help me save them."

She slowly pulled her hands from mine and rubbed them up and down her bare arms. "I . . . I don't know. They took all my weapons from me, I can't even protect myself."

It took everything I had not to yell at her, to try and force her into coming, but I knew it wouldn't work. I had to convince her I was on her side, show her I trusted her even when I didn't. I dropped to a crouch and dug into my bag. I pulled out a silver-edged knife with a six-inch blade. "Take it, use it if you have to. The silver will cut through any supernatural."

Carefully she took the knife and tucked it into her belt. "You don't even know my name."

Time to roll the dice. "Tell me your name when you're ready to save these boys. We'll wait for you at the bakery over there as long as we can," I said, and Levi held the phone up again for her, showing her the triplets once more.

She backed away, her eyes locked on the image. I didn't move until I couldn't see her any longer.

"Liam, what are we going to do?" Levi asked.

"Exactly what I said." I glanced at him. "We're going to wait for her at the bakery and hope to all that is holy she shows up in the next few hours."

I slung my bag back up over my shoulder and headed toward the growing scent of fresh bread and pastries.

"Have you been there before?" Levi asked.

"No."

"How do you know where you are going, then?"

I touched the tip of my nose. "I can smell it."

"Wow. That's cool. Do you think I'll be able to smell stuff like that?" He looked down at the palm of his hand, but no water appeared. I shrugged.

"I don't know. Elemental magic isn't the same as supernatural. Like I said, Nigel is the one you want to talk to about it." I picked up my pace, which kept him from asking more questions. Half an hour later, we were in front of the dark windows of Vanilla and Honey. A Greek specialty bakery, if the sign was correct. By the smells, though the windows were dark, the bakery was in full swing in the back. My stomach rumbled, but there was nothing I could do for it at the moment. It had to wait too.

I made my way around the side and found a shadowed recess against the building to tuck into. "You might as well try and sleep." I pointed to the step and Levi didn't argue. He sat and pulled his jacket up around his ears. Moments later, his heartbeat slowed along with his breathing as he slipped into dreamland.

The fact that he could crash in such an uncomfortable position made me think he'd slept more than one night on the street in order to keep away from his father. I shook my head, hard pressed to understand why a man would do that to his own child. There was no reason I could see that would ever make me turn away from any of my kids. Or any of my pack for that matter.

I kept watch, noting the cars that came and went, none of them passing more than once. We weren't being watched, which was a good thing, a small good thing considering everything. The slowly shifting light as the moon sank further through the sky made my shoulders tighten with anxiety. How long did the ogre need to decide if she would help us or not?

Four a.m. came and went, and a few people drifted into the bakery for their coffee and sugar-laden breakfasts. Five a.m. rolled around and I began to doubt. No, she had to come, she had to, there was no other choice.

Six a.m. and the moon set, the sun rose above the edge of the world, and a dim light grew around us. We were down to thirty-seven hours. I adjusted my stance, watching, knowing that while I'd told the female ogre we could only wait so long, I was not being entirely honest. I wanted to believe there would be other females, but . . . I wasn't sure. And then there was something about this ogre that stuck with me. The wolf in me bobbed his head in agreement. This was the female we needed.

End of story.

Which meant I would wait, and if she didn't come, I would go looking for her.

The faint scent of milk and ogre wafted down the alley. I stood straighter and took a few steps to the edge of the building. There she was, but with her was a big-ass male ogre. His skin was as dark as hers, minus the purple splattering, and he was speaking in low tones.

"You aren't listening to me, stupid chit," he snarled. "I am trying to save you."

"No, you're not. You're going to sell me out to them. I'm one of the last females this tribe has, and you don't want to lose a warm body that isn't one of your boyfriend fuck buddies."

He grabbed her arm. "You can have another child, but not if you're dead. The council is speaking right now and unless I stand for you, they're going to kill you this time, and not just beat you." He leaned into her. "What did you think you were doing, getting knocked up by Tul when you were supposed to be bedding Pic? Did you think they would just let you go?"

She jerked her arm away from him. "And if you speak for me? What does that cost, Buk?"

"You'll bed who I say, when I say. You know the rules. You'll belong to me, you will be my property. I will take responsibility for you." She shoved him and he stumbled past the alley opening as he struggled to gain his balance.

I reached out from the shadows and grabbed his one flailing arm. I yanked him into the alley with me, not thinking much about anything but doing as I'd told her I would. I would protect her from her own kind and everything else that came her way. I snapped his arm up behind his back, spun him to the ground, and slammed his face into the concrete. I put a knee into the center of his back and kept the sharp angle of his arm twisted high. "I think you should listen to her."

"Who the fuck do you think you are?" He took a big sniff. "Fucking piece of dog shit wolf. I'm going to skin you alive and eat your balls for breakfast." I grabbed a handful of his hair and yanked his head back, then smashed it into the ground.

"Now, that isn't very polite, is it? Play nice." I slapped the back of his head, which pushed his nose into the concrete again. He howled, and I glanced over my shoulder. "What do you want to do with him?" Below me the ogre twisted and tried to buck me off which forced me to look away from her for a moment. When I looked back, she was striding forward, a grim look on her face, one I'd seen more than once on an ogre. She was in fight mode. Shit.

She pulled the knife I'd given her from her

waistband in a single smooth motion that told me she knew how to use it. Flipping the handle around, she had it angled downward for a deadly blow. For just a moment, I thought I'd judged her wrong. That the blade would come at me.

With a wicked thrust, she drove the knife through the back of the male ogre's head. He jerked once, twice, and then was still. Breathing hard, she crouched beside me and held out her hand. "My name is Mai."

I took her hand. "Liam." Even though I had already introduced myself, it felt right. "And the kid over there is Levi."

Levi didn't even move, he was still sound asleep despite the scuffle. I shook my head. I shouldn't have been surprised, we'd been running on adrenaline and not much else since we left home. With Mai's help, I dragged the dead ogre to the closest dumpster and shoved his body in. We dropped the lid with a slam.

"That won't buy us much time," she said. "A few hours at most."

"We won't need that much time to . . ." I stared at her face, seeing the indecision there. "What?"

She tucked the knife back into her belt. "I can't leave yet. I have to go back to my apartment first."

"If what I overheard is right, that's not a good idea. We have to go now and use the time we have on our side."

Mai drew a breath. "My son's ashes are there. I can't leave without him. Surely you can understand that?"

I closed my eyes and pinched the bridge of my nose, thinking it through. "How long?"

"My place is in Redmond, about an hour by transit."

"What about a cab? That would be faster." There had to be a way to speed this up.

"No, they're watching the cabs. Apparently there were a few supernaturals that infiltrated using cabs last week."

That would be Rylee again. Damn it. I nodded. "Okay. I'm coming with you."

"No, you stink to high heaven like an alpha wolf. They'll pick up on you in no time. You can't come with me. I have to go alone."

"I could go with her," Levi said, finally joining the conversation, cautiously, like he wasn't sure he was welcome. "I don't smell, do I?"

Her eyes shot to him. "Are you a supernatural?"

He held out his hand and water pooled in his palm, the same as the night before. His voice held more than a little pride to it as he spoke. "Elemental."

Slowly she nodded even while I struggled not to strangle Levi. Against an ogre, he had no chance. No shot. She drew a big sniff of his hair, making it ruffle toward her nose. "He doesn't smell like anything. And if he can manipulate water he could be an asset."

"No. We don't split up," I said. "Right now, we have the advantage and it will cut time if we go together. We can leave from your apartment."

Her jaw twitched, a flash of anger there, defiance.

I held up my hands. "I'm not trying to control you. I used to be a cop. I bossed people around for a living." I winked at her, softening what I was saying. I hoped.

She let out a sigh. "I hate that you're right."

"Don't get used to it. My mate is right more than me."

The three of us stepped onto the sidewalk. To my right, Levi's stomach let out a growl that made my wolf twitch and whine with agreement. I paused at the door to the bakery.

"Give me two minutes." I stepped in, and ordered up a mixed bag of pastries and three large coffees. The lady at the counter was quiet, her eyes downcast.

"Thanks," I said as I took the bag and my change.

"Don't hurt her," she said.

Now that stopped my feet. "Excuse me?"

The woman looked up, brown eyes full of determination that I wouldn't have expected from such a quiet mouse of a girl. "Mai is my friend. She's been through a lot, losing her son and her husband going missing. Don't hurt her. Please."

I nodded, glad for the additional information. "I'm not going to hurt her. I'm going to get her out of this town."

She let out a sigh of relief. "Then the breakfast is on me." She handed me back my twenty-dollar bill. "Tell her Alena wishes her luck. I think things will get better for her if she goes with you."

I reached across the counter and shook her hand. "You got it, Alena of Vanilla and Honey."

She smiled, a blush spreading over her pale cheeks. "Thank you."

I strode out of the shop and handed out the coffees. As we walked, I told Mai what Alena had said. She smiled, but it was sad. "She's a nice girl, but I think she should keep the luck for herself. Her life is hardly an easy one."

She continued to talk about her friend, but I zoned out, instead focusing on the situation around us. Mai didn't notice, but we were slowly being surrounded by ogres. A bus pulled up to a stop about ten feet in front of us, and I hurried Mai and Levi forward. "Onto the bus, now."

"It's going the wrong direction," Mai spluttered, and then she looked behind us and gasped. She leapt onto the bus and I shoved Levi on behind her. "Go. Levi, take her to where Ophelia dropped us when you get what you need. Get her back to Rylee, understand? No matter what." I handed them the bag of weapons, taking only two out for myself. A short sword and an oversized curved skinning knife I could hold with a fist.

"Wait, what are you doing?" Levi yelled.

"Buying you time," I said. "Keep her safe, Levi."

The look on his face shifted from fear to determination and he nodded. "I will."

The bus door shut behind them and the driver pulled away, maybe sensing it would be best for his vehicle to get its ass in gear.

"Well, well. A wolf in sheep's clothing perhaps?"

I turned to face a black-skinned ogre who stood at least eight feet tall. "No, a wolf in wolf's clothing."

CHAPTER 5

"MY NAME IS Pic, and I am the leader of this territory." The ogre that I'd pegged at eight feet took a few more steps in my direction. Make that nine feet tall and easily three feet across the shoulders. He pulled a large sword from his back, the blade splitting at the handle into two blades. He took a lazy swing with it in my direction but I didn't move. I knew a bluff move when I saw one. "Are you not going to introduce yourself?"

I shrugged and did a lazy loop with my own weapon. "Nah. You win. Your sword is bigger than mine."

The other ogres all laughed, guffawing. Dick humor, nothing new there.

Pic grinned. "I almost hate to kill you with a sense of humor like that. But you were with one of our females. That is not allowed. I would hate to see what a cross-species wolf/ogre would look like. Besides weak."

I shrugged. "Accidental meeting. I wanted on the bus, she beat me to it. Besides, I thought you killed everything that moved in your territory?"

"We do. But we have uses for some supernaturals. As we have uses for some humans." He snapped his fingers and several police officers slid between the ogre ranks, guns raised.

Shit running down my legs couldn't have been more

shocking. Rylee had told me the ogres had humans working for them, but it was still surprising.

He circled around me and I moved with him, keeping him in front of me. A part of my brain flat out revolted at what was happening. I mean, we were in Seattle, in broad daylight, humans walking past us like this wasn't even happening. What the actual fuck was going on?

"You wouldn't want to hurt the nice police officers, now, would you? You're probably one of those supernaturals who tries to keep them alive, aren't you?" Pic taunted and the other ogres laughed. But they backed off, giving the cops free rein to move in.

I didn't get a chance to try and talk my way out of things.

The first cop squeezed off a round that slammed into my belly. I dropped to my knees, shock making me slow for two reasons.

One was the simple fact that the cops were so under the ogres' control that they would shoot without just cause. Two, that the gun actually worked around this many supernaturals which took my brain to a place I didn't want to go. What if the weapons Rylee and I thought we'd destroyed a while back had survived? If those guns were now in the hands of the ogre tribe here in Seattle, that would be bad on so, so many levels.

Three more shots ripped through the air before I could move, one hitting me in the heart, the second in the hip, the third . . . I blanked out before I could tell where it struck.

Lights out for Liam.

Darkness and pain were all my brain could register as I came around. That and I was folded over on myself, my head shoved between my knees like some sort of twisted yoga pose.

Praying for mercy.

Slowly my senses came back online. The smell of rotting food, shit, and vomit slithered up my nose and I sneezed, but that only cleared my sinuses for more of the scent. I groaned and my back cracked and popped, vertebrae aching as I sat up. Blinking, I looked around, tried to get my bearings as my nose took in the strong scent of ogre under all the other scents. That froze me where I was, stilling the breath in my lungs. Maybe they hadn't seen me yet. Maybe I had a chance to get the drop on them. There were walls around me, dark blue and close enough that I could reach out and touch them if I'd wanted. My brain didn't register, couldn't seem to grasp where I was. Only that the smell of ogre meant danger.

I pulled myself up slowly and under my ass something shifted like sand and rocks giving way. I looked down at the back of the head of the ogre Mai had killed. Blood and gray matter had coagulated underneath me. I grimaced at the smell and the memories came back to me, the bits of the past few hours slipping back into place.

Pic and his mob had stuffed me in the same Dumpster as Buk, the bastard that had tried to become Mai's pimp. Nice. I grabbed the edge of the Dumpster and heaved myself out. There were no other ogres besides the dead one, which was a small blessing. I gave myself a full body shake and three of the four bullets that had been shot into me fell to the cement with a tinny clatter. My head throbbed with a dull ache, like a hangover from ogre beer. I put a hand to my right temple, just as the bullet pushed its way out.

"Well, that answers that question," I grumbled, staring at the bullet. So, apparently, I could take a hit to the head, but I wasn't sure I wanted to repeat that particular experience.

I took a look at the skyline, but couldn't see the sun past the buildings that rose around me. It didn't feel like much time had passed, but that could just be the loss of time from the injury to my head.

I shook myself again and did a slow turn. Pic and his buddies had taken my two weapons, and I was covered in filth from the Dumpster. Not just blood and brain matter from Buk's wounds, but rotten food, and spoiled meat. I felt around for my back pocket, looking for my leather wallet. My fingers found nothing but empty space. I scrubbed both hands over my face despite the grime that covered both face and hands. I needed to think this through and fast. There weren't a lot of choices left.

If I could shift into my wolf form, I could cover the distance to Redmond in no time, catch up to Levi and Mai and get the three of us the fuck out of here. Right now, Pic and his mob thought I was dead, which meant they wouldn't be looking for me. As long as I could keep clear of them, I had the upper hand.

I closed my eyes and reluctantly tried to call my wolf forward. How the hell I was going to shift while I was using Faris's body was beyond me. Would I be a white wolf now, instead of the black shaggy beast I'd been before? Would my eyes be bluer yet? Would I be smaller, like a leaner version of what I knew to be my wolf?

The questions flowed through me in rapid succession, over and over, making me sweat with the possibilities.

My wolf ignored me, essentially curling up in the corner of my mind and going to sleep. What the hell.

"Shithead," I muttered. So much for calling on innate abilities.

Warily, I made my way to the edge of the alley and peered out. Not an ogre in sight, nor any scent on the wind. I didn't even know anyone in Seattle, not even old FBI contacts that I could reach out to. See if I could get a little help.

To my right, the soft ding of a door being opened drew my attention to the bakery.

Maybe there *was* someone who could help me. I went into the bakery, the smell of sugar and fresh-baked bread making my stomach grumble loudly. The coffee had been too long ago between the fight, injuries, and healing. The three customers who stood in the store turned at the same time, but the reactions were a ripple effect. I caught a glimpse of myself in the mirrored glass of the display cases. Yes, I could see why they would be concerned. I was covered in filth, blood smeared my white shirt in several places, and my head was sticky with blood. Not exactly the look you want in a guy around your baked goods. I looked past the gasps and surprised eyes to the brown-eyed, brown-haired cashier.

"You said you were Mai's friend. Is that true?" I asked.

"What happened to you?" She came around the counter, her eyes as big and round as the customers'. Seriously, I was getting irritated with all the surprise. Then again, most of the people I was dealing with didn't know much about the supernatural, so it made sense there would be a fair amount of shock around me. I suddenly felt bad for all the questions and shit I'd put Rylee through in the beginning. And for all the wide and rolled eyes I'd given her when I didn't believe what had come out of her mouth.

I cleared my throat. "Can we speak in private?"

She waved a hand behind her. "Diana, can you come and run the cash register?"

Another woman who looked to be in her late thirties came out of the back, took one look at me and pointedly looked at the customers. I followed Mai's friend into the back of the bakery. She pointed at a chair. "Sit. You look like you're going to fall over."

"Alena, right?"

She nodded. "Yes. What happened? Should I call the police? Or maybe an ambulance?"

"No. No police. They, the police that is, did this to me. Look, I need to get to Mai's apartment, but . . ."

"You don't know where it is?"

I nodded. "They took everything I had on me,

including my wallet." I had to grit my teeth over asking for help from a complete stranger. I knew what I sounded like. A scam artist. I lost my wallet, I just need to get to a friend's and I'll pay you back. Just loan me a few bucks, I'm getting paid later this week. I'd heard it all and then some from my own family as much as the people I'd dealt with on the job. I could only hope that Alena hadn't been scammed in her short life, and that she was a bit naïve to the ways of the world.

Because there was no way I could get to Redmond and find Mai and Levi without her help. Not if I was going to stay ahead of Pic and his mob.

Biting back every ounce of pride I had, I spoke. "Can you give me a ride?"

Her eyebrows shot to her hairline. "No, my husband wouldn't like that. It wouldn't be proper." She reached over the desk and grabbed a set of keys. "But because you are Mai's friend . . . you can take my car."

Okay, so beyond naïve? Was that even a thing? Or maybe she was just that kind. I chose to believe the latter. Kindness to that level was going to get her in trouble at some point. Mai had been right about that.

She gave me the keys. "Park it at the back of Mai's apartment and leave the keys inside the muffler. I'll get a ride out after work and pick it up."

"Thank you," I said, glad that Mai had at least one person looking out for her.

"Just help her. Obviously," she waved a hand at me, "you are having a rough day and I can tell you are trying to help her. In your own way. I can sense these things, you know." She scribbled something on a pad of paper and tore the top sheet off, handing it to me. "Mai's address."

I took the keys and paper, and she pointed to the back door. "Brown hatchback. It isn't much, but it'll get you there."

"Again. Thank you."

"Just help her. She deserves a little happiness," she said softly. Like maybe Mai wasn't the only one who deserved a little joy.

I wondered as I walked out the door at the kind of person who would hand over keys to their vehicle to a veritable stranger on their word that they were going to help one of their friends. I hoped that helping me didn't get her into trouble with the ogre mob. And I hoped she managed to keep that willingness to help those around her. It would be a shame to see her lose that—the world needed more people like Alena.

I jogged to the hatchback and slid into the tiny, beat-up car. The age of the vehicle was in my favor. Anything newer and I wasn't sure it would have started for me. Thankfully, the engine turned over and I was off and running. I followed the signs that directed me toward Redmond without a single ogre coming into view. Two cop cars passed me. But they didn't so much as look in my direction, though I felt myself cringing as they went by. Which made me think of Levi and the way he cringed and hunched his back—afraid to be hurt.

I glanced several times at the piece of paper Mai's friend had written on, making sure I had the directions right. The apartment building was on Heritage Street. Fourth floor up according to the instructions.

Thirty-five minutes later, I did a slow drive by the building with 6800 lettered on the side in fake gold. At the front doors were two ogres posing as doormen. They held the glass doors open for those going in and out, but I had no doubt they were there for an entirely different reason. As in keeping Mai and Levi either in or out.

Fuck it all. I smacked the steering wheel with one hand in a steady rhythm as I tried to formulate a plan that might actually work. But there was no way I could get past two ogres on my own without them alerting the rest of their group.

I did a loop around the block to get a look at the back of the building. There it was, a back door. Another ogre in front of it, but only one. That was going to be my best shot at things unless . . . I backed up and parked a half block away from the east side of the building. Balconies ran all the way up this side of the building and below them all . . . was a small service door.

The service door probably had an ogre lurking around somewhere. I wasn't going to bank on them not covering all their bases. As Ophelia had pointed out, they weren't stupid.

I scratched at my chin, knowing I had to look at this logically. The humans with the ogres had guns that could pin me down, that much I knew. And if they all figured out that I was a Guardian, I had no doubt they'd figure out that killing me would take a simple removing of my head from shoulders.

All that meant nothing at the moment. I needed to get in that damn apartment and either get Levi and Mai out, or wait for them to show. No matter which plan it ended up being, it started with me being stealthy and quiet.

Rylee would have laughed her ass off at me for the situation I was in. Stealthy and quiet were not something either of us did well on a good day.

"Get moving," I growled at myself, and stepped out of the hatchback. I shut it and slid around the back, placing the keys inside the half-rotted-out muffler. Actually, it wasn't a bad hiding spot. Unless you were looking to fix the little car, you might not even notice the muffler, never mind the keys inside it. I approached the building, drawing in deep breaths, scenting the air with each step. Ogre, the musk was heavy on the cool breeze, but no scent of Mai or Levi. Of course, they probably went in the front door. Assuming they were already here and made it in before the cavalry showed up.

Going through the front door wasn't something I had the luxury of doing. Small, tiny side door and hoping for a very light guard on it. As I drew closer to the service door, a cop stood from where he'd been sitting in the stairwell.

"Excuse me, I'm turned around here." I used Levi's excuse. The cop shook his head.

"Front door is around there." He thumbed to one side and I kept closing the distance between us.

"Which way?" I tipped my head as if I hadn't heard him, or was too stupid to understand a simple sentence. He let out an exasperated sigh.

"Fucking druggies. Get out of here." He shooed at me with both hands, like a stray dog.

I grinned, and he went pale. I closed the distance between us in a single leap. His face drew a startled look and then he was under me as I thumped a fist into his jaw. The crack of bone didn't bother me. I recognized him from my shooting on the street: he'd been the one to shoot me in the heart.

I yanked the gun from his belt and turned it over in my hand while I strangled him with the other. The gun was not exactly like the ones that Rylee and I had destroyed. But it was obvious there was magic about it. I flipped open the chamber with my thumb and peered in. There were small round balls of steel, and behind them was a glittering, rolling twist of green magic. It looked like bullets were propelled through the barrel by magic, not gunpowder. Fuck, it was brilliant and terrifying. Magical guns were not something this world needed in the state it was currently in. Or ever, for that matter. That being said, I wasn't going to leave it behind.

I tucked the weapon into the back of my jeans and frisked the cop. I took a baton off him, and his radio which I clipped to my shirt and it immediately crackled and blipped off. Shit. I yanked it off and threw it on the ground where it bounced once and then came back to life with a click. Piece of shit technology. I found one more magazine of ammo on the cop, and tucked it into the back pocket of my jeans.

I flipped him over and used his handcuffs on him, and a piece of his shirt to gag him. He was out cold at the moment, but that could change. I dragged him away from the stairwell and stuffed him into a large hydrangea bush that grew high above my head. Yes, I knew what kind of flowering bush it was, because it was a memory of Faris's that gave me the species. I shook my head and went down the stairwell. Behind me the radio came to life. "Bartlett. Status? Any sign of Mai or the kid?"

I broke off a branch from the bush and walked over to the radio. I managed to depress the call button, stretched as far from it as I could be. "Negative."

The radio squelched and then came back to life. "What the fuck, Bart, you get a cold?"

"Frog in my throat," I growled.

The radio went quiet and my ears perked at the sound of feet coming around the corner of the building. Fucking lady luck was not on my side, the fickle bitch.

I flattened my back against the door and drew a slow breath, calming my heart as I kept the gun steady in my right hand. Left, I was a lefty. But Faris was right-handed. I switched hands and waited, irritation flowing through me. There was an intake of breath and I leaned out to see another cop peering into the hydrangea bush. The cop I'd stuffed in there had wiggled out a single leg in the short time. Which was going to work in my favor, since he kept his buddy distracted.

"Fuck, Bartlett, what happened?"

He bent over his buddy and I slipped up behind him. I tucked the gun away and pulled the baton out. I slid it in front his neck and pulled back with a sharp yank. With a scrambled squawk, he fought the baton, but I held it easily. These cops might have guns that could work against me. But the shits didn't have a chance against my speed and strength even if my wolf was currently ignoring me.

Slowly he relaxed, maybe slumped is a better word, and I let him go before his heart stopped. I didn't really want to kill them. I'd been one of them not so long ago, and I couldn't help myself in wanting to believe they could change for the better. I dropped him next to Bartlett and didn't bother to tie him up. I did, however, take his gun and extra ammo, along with the flak jacket he wore, which I slipped on over my torn-up shirt. Things were going downhill, I might as well try and be as prepared as I could.

I ran to the door, and didn't slow. I slammed my foot onto the door handle and the steel door gave way with a groan. So much for stealthy and quiet.

Inside the stairwell, I did a quick sweep, holding both guns out. I didn't want to admit it, but having a gun in both hands felt more natural than any sword, any crossbow. This was how I'd been trained to deal with the bad guys.

The radio squawked to life again behind me on the grass. "What the fuck are you boys doing back there?"

I looked over my shoulder, and then approached the radio. Using the baton, I pressed the call button. "In pursuit of suspects. North end of Heritage."

"Affirmative. Backup on its way."

Bingo. I'd sent them on a goose chase, but the radio would only take me so far.

I swept up the stairs, guns held at the ready, fully expecting a herd of ogres to rush me. I made it all the way to the fourth floor before I heard any sound of pursuit.

"Where'd he go?"

"Only way to go is up, you dumb shit."

The two voices echoed up to me from the bottom of the stairwell as I slipped through the door that led onto Mai's level.

The two voices sounded like Bartlett and his friend. So the boys were awake, then. Not that I was much worried about them. They would be easily dealt with again, if needed.

I looked down one length of the hall, then the other. No ogres here, but there was a faint scent of Mai and Levi which made me perk up. I followed my quarry down to room 456, which according to the paper from Alena was Mai's apartment. I knocked on the door with the back of one hand and lowered my voice. "Mai. It's Liam."

There was no answer. I took a few steps, considering breaking the door down, but decided against it. I drew in a breath, picking up on their scents and working backward to the elevators. There it was, they'd backtracked in order to throw the other ogres off. But my nose wouldn't be fooled. I wonder if she knew that?

I pressed the call button on the elevator. They would have gone up, away from the ogres searching them out. I pulled both guns and trained them on the elevator as the doors slid open. Just in case.

My caution was not needed this time, though. The elevator dinged open, empty, but still I hesitated for a brief moment before getting on. I had to believe it wouldn't fall out from under me. Even if it felt totally unnatural to ride the elevator, it was only because of what technology could, and most often would, do around me. Then again, the stairwell was likely flooding with ogres. They wouldn't expect me to take the lift.

The door slid shut and soft music piped through the vents. I held still in the middle of the elevator, legs braced apart and guns still in my hands. I hit all the buttons on the elevator above me, all seven. Each floor opened up and I peered out, taking a breath of air. No Mai or Levi on the floor above. Or the next. But on the seventh floor, Levi's scent tugged at me.

"What the hell are you two nincompoops doing splitting up?" I growled, pissed that I had to go after him first. Much as I didn't want the kid to get hurt, I needed to get Mai back to Rylee. If I had to leave Levi behind and come back to Seattle to get him, I would. Yet the wolf in me drove me forward, forcing me to get the kid, too.

Pack, the kid was part of my pack now, and you

didn't leave pack members behind. Even when they were being idiots.

I stepped off the elevator and hurried down the hall, following the growing smell of the kid until I stopped in front of a cleaning cabinet. I tucked one gun into my belt and jerked the door open. Levi stood there, hands out, water dripping from them.

"Shit. Liam, you found me!" he gasped and lowered his hands.

"Wasn't a game of hide and seek, kid." I grabbed him by the shoulder and yanked him out. "Where is Mai?"

"I don't know. She pushed me out here and told me to hide."

I tipped my head for him to follow me and we hurried back to the elevator. I hit the call button.

The problem with elevators in my estimation was that when they weren't slow, they were often full and you couldn't take them. In this particular case, I wished the damn thing had only been slow and not full of three seriously pissed off, bloodthirsty ogres.

CHAPTER 6

WHAT I DIDN'T expect was Levi stepping in front of me, his hands outstretched, water dripping from them. The ogres laughed, and I fully admit I almost did too. Until the water shot so hard from the kid that he slammed backward into me with the force of it. I held him as water flooded the elevator, like a tiny aquarium filled with floating ogres that apparently hadn't thought the kid was a threat. Hell, *I* hadn't thought the kid was a threat.

They swam forward as if they were going to get out, but they couldn't break through the water. Levi held his hands out, his arms shaking. "I don't know how long I can hold them."

I lifted my gun that I still gripped in my right hand and squeezed off three quick rounds, taking them each in the head. Red flowering blooms filled the water, quickly darkening the space.

"Why did you do that? I had them," Levi asked, immediately contradicting himself. I lowered the gun, thinking only of the innocence I'd had to take from Pamela so young. Asking her to kill me, to give Rylee time to give birth to Marcella in safety. Asking Pamela to fight at our sides when she was still only a child, when she should have been thinking about going to prom and dreaming about having a pony. Not thinking about how to kill her enemies, how to train so that she could help us stop demons, or what was the best way to fend off those who wanted to manipulate and use her for her incredible strength.

"Trust me, you don't want to have lives on your conscience any sooner than you have to. Because the day will come that you will have to. I just hope it isn't today." I strode forward, reached into the elevator and hit the full stop button. The door slid shut as I stepped away. "That's only going to buy us a little time."

"I think she went up further."

I didn't roll my eyes at Levi spitting out the obvious. There was no experience in him, and he was getting a crash course. "How did you figure out the water?" It was my turn for a question or two. "And what happened that you two split up?"

"The ogres followed us, and we got off at the next bus stop because Mai said she had a place we could hide for a bit. From what she told me, she's been hiding out from them for longer than just a few days. A few months at least. They caught her and her son a few weeks ago. He wasn't very old, Liam."

I pushed away the sympathetic grief that came from those words. No time for feelings, no time for emotions.

I nodded, and he went on. "The thing was, there was an ogre waiting for us at the hiding place. He didn't seem all that mean, though, seeing as Mai kissed him. And he told her to get to her apartment. He said he had been able to convince the council that she wasn't in the city, but he was sure Pic knew he was lying. And then he told her that she needed to get out of town, to get as far away as she could."

"So she has one person on her side."

He nodded. "I think so. He gave her a set of keys and we took his truck here. But there were already ogres on the front door so we slipped in the back. They hadn't covered it yet."

That made sense. Cops were always late to the game when it wasn't urgent. "And then?"

"We went to her apartment and she got her amulet, she said she had her son's ashes put into the amber, and she grabbed a small bag of things. That's when we heard the other ogres. Or she did, to be fair." He shrugged his thin shoulders and I gestured for him to get behind me. We were at the door to the stairwell. I pressed my ear against it, and nothing came back, no echo of feet or heartbeats. I put a finger to my lips and eased the door open. The smell of ogre was thick like smoke, but there weren't any actually in the stairwell. Though, it hadn't been long since they'd been there. I slid in and Levi followed.

The door slammed behind him and I whipped around, glaring at him. He mouthed "sorry," and I had to restrain myself from shaking him. A good shake might have sent him to his knees, and we didn't have time for me to try and make right any impulsive behavior.

Time to hurry, not time to discipline.

I ran up the stairs, light on my feet, not a sound from the steps. Levi clomped up behind me, breathing hard. I struggled not to growl at him. That bothered my wolf more than me asking for a shift in form. The wolf in me wanted me to show patience to a pup, to show him how to hunt and lead. Again, this was not the time for that. Later, if we made it out of this alive.

Because I wasn't so sure that was going to be a possibility with the way things were going so far.

I opened the door on the eighth floor. No scent of Mai. I shook my head, knowing we were wasting time. Where would I go if I were being driven through the building? High, I'd go for high ground.

"We're going to the roof," I said.

"How do you know she's there?" Levi asked, and at least this time he kept his voice down.

"I don't. But it's where I would go. She might be able to scale down a side they aren't watching, or if the buildings are close enough, she might be able to jump between them."

"The buildings are way too far apart," Levi said. "There's no way she could jump them."

I shook my head and kept my mouth shut. Levi was about to be fully inducted into the world of the supernatural. It was better he saw things rather than only be told. Most of what our world offered was hard to believe on a good day, never mind on a day when you'd been shot at, chased, and learned you could shoot water out of the palms of your hands.

Not normal, not easy to take in, but life just the same.

I raced up the stairs, letting Levi come at his own pace, leaving him behind.

Which was a mistake.

He was a floor below me when the ogres burst out right behind him. "Liam!"

I spun and saw the ogres as they launched toward him. I lifted my gun and squeezed off a round, nailing the ogre closest to Levi in the shoulder. The big brute spun backward and took out the ogres behind him like a big fat set of dominos.

"Hurry your ass up, kid."

Suddenly, Levi was beside me, step for step. Mind you, his face was white as a new sheet of paper and his breathing was ragged enough that I figured if he hyperventilated much more, he'd pass out. We reached the top floor just as his legs wobbled and his eyes rolled back in his head. I caught him around the waist and helped him through the door. I set him off to one side, turned, and threw the deadbolt lock on the door. Beside Levi was a large concrete planter. I tucked my gun behind my belt and grabbed the edges of the planter. Maybe it would give us an extra few minutes if we were lucky. One could hope.

As I grasped the edge of the planter, I noticed a handprint on it, bright red and wet. The scent of Mai hit me along with the smell of blood. That was not good. She was injured and stumbling. I could almost see her fall out of the door and use the planter to right herself before hurrying onward.

The gravel shrieked as I dragged the concrete planter across it. I got it against the door just as the first blow hit the steel. I grabbed Levi's arm and hauled him up.

"Time to find Mai and get the fuck out of here."

He said nothing as I pulled him along behind me. After a few steps, he got his feet under himself and he shook me off. "I'm good. I'm good."

I said nothing, only kept my attention on the smell of a wounded Mai. "Mai!"

There was no answer, of course not. Her scent trail led to the edge of the roof. I looked over the edge, searching for more bloody handprints.

"Did she jump?" Levi asked.

There were no prints that showed her scaling down the building.

"Not like you're thinking." I pointed to the building across from us. It was about four floors lower than the one we stood on, and easily forty feet away. Forty. There was a scuff in the roof that looked like hands and feet imprints to me. "She jumped across there, and we have to follow her."

"Are you crazy?"

I glanced at him. "No. I'm not. But I can't leave you here because those assholes know you're with me and Mai now. And that does not bode well for you."

"I can hide," he said. "I'm good at hiding."

"This isn't like your dad, Levi. Hiding won't work. They've got your scent." I shook my head.

He swallowed hard. "Then how are we going to get across there?"

I grinned at him, the wolf in me surfacing a little, liking that what I was going to say would make him squirm.

"Remember the zoo fence?" I asked.

He groaned. "Are you serious?"

I pointed at the far building. "I'm going to boost you. Get back there, close to the door, and then run at me with all you've got. I can throw you across, but only if you're going full speed."

"You're serious?" he squeaked again, and behind him the door echoed his sentiment.

"No time to argue. You've got elemental blood in you. You're tougher than you look, so this is not going to hurt like you think. Trust me." In other words, hurry your ass up, kid. I need you to trust me or we're both going to die, and I can't leave you here and just save myself. A pack doesn't work like that.

He backed away about twenty feet and I crouched at the edge of the roof. "Get your foot on my leg here, where my hands are. We've got one shot at this."

Levi's jaw tightened, and a wave of determination seemed to roll over him. He bolted toward me, timing his step and jump just right.

As his foot touched down on my leg and cupped hands, I stood, using the strength in my limbs to vault him over my head. I didn't even look to see if he made it; he was free flying now. I turned and backed up, prepping my own run. The door behind me burst open and the ogres spilled onto the roof like a disturbed ant nest as they hurried to get around me. Fuck, I couldn't even count how many there were. But Pic was there at the front of the group. "I thought we killed you."

"Surprise." I flipped them off and ran for the ledge of the building. I got my foot on the edge and pushed off as hard as I could, arms pinwheeling as if that would somehow help me across the distance.

The sound of guns going off popped through the air. I was hit twice in the back and spun sideways as I fell. Grateful for the flak jacket, I knew it wasn't going to help me if I hit the ground from this height. Survive I might, but badly injured I would be. And then I'd be at the mercy of the ogres who wouldn't just throw me in a Dumpster this time. I knew that much.

This all went through my head in the split second I spun and fell toward the far building. I saw a flash of Levi's big eyes as I missed the roof of the building he stood on. Calm flowed through me. I wasn't done yet.

I reached out and caught the window ledge as it whipped by me. My body snapped hard with the sudden stop, yanking my shoulder from its socket, pulling at muscles and tendons, tearing through several. But I stopped myself. Actually, I slammed into the brick building so hard, the blow knocked the wind out of me. More gunshots rattled off the building around me, the impacts spraying concrete and dust as the bullets bit into the wall.

Hanging there, I pulled one gun and aimed it at an ogre standing at the edge of the far building. I pulled the trigger, he screamed and fell over the side. I shot two more before they backed off. I tucked the gun away and climbed up the wall, using the divots from the projectiles as well as the window ledge. Difficult with one good arm, but manageable. I got to the top and flopped over the edge. I put my shoulder back in its socket, hard and fast before I could think about how much it was going to hurt. The tendons and muscles were already knitting back together. At least I had that much going for me.

Levi squatted beside me. "Holy shit, you hit them! How come they couldn't hit you and you could hit them?"

"Because they can't aim worth shit and I'm a marksman. Top of my class," I grumbled as I sat, breathing hard and letting my body have a minute to heal before I got up.

Faris's body would have some new scars after this little adventure. I shook my head, more rattled than I cared to admit.

I forced myself to pull it together and drew in a breath, finding Mai's scent easily. "She went this way." I stood and broke into a jog, following Mai to the other side of the building. But . . . I backed up a few steps. She'd backtracked again. I followed her backwards. "Clever girl." I ran back to the edge of the building. All the ogres were gone from Mai's apartment building and currently swarming across the street toward this one. My mind put the pieces together and I couldn't help smiling. "Mai, you clever, clever ogre. I am glad you're going to work with me, and not against me."

"Why would you say that?" Levi asked.

I pointed at the blood spots and scuff marks. "'Cause she's damn smart. She leapt back to her apartment building after leading a scent trail as if she hopped to the next one."

Levi groaned. "Tell me we aren't jumping back."

I grinned at him. "All right, I won't tell you. But only because you already know it." I grabbed him by the shoulder. "Ready?"

"If I say no, does that change anything?"

I laughed. "Nope."

CHAPTER 7

THE JUMP BACK to Mai's apartment building went as fine as a forty-foot jump with a twenty-foot drop can go. Mai's apartment was higher, but there was no way we were going to hit the roof. As it was, we dropped a solid twenty-five feet and ended up landing on the second floor. I tossed Levi and managed to land him on a larger balcony, right on a lounge chair that crumpled under his weight. I was able to land so I ended up hanging from the same balcony, but this time I was ready for the sudden stop and didn't pop either of my shoulders out.

We slipped through the sliding glass door and into the apartment of an older gentleman who didn't even look up as we passed behind him. His eyes were glued to the TV; a hockey game was playing. As if he were with them on the ice, he flinched and bobbed along with the players as they battled back and forth. To be that oblivious to the world around you, I wasn't sure if it was a blessing or a curse.

We let ourselves out into the hallway, and I knew where we were headed. The backtrack method . . . if she stuck with it, we would find her at her apartment, I was sure of it.

We made it to the fourth floor with no problem, though we passed a trio of grumbling maintenance men as they headed toward the seventh floor and the jammed elevator.

Levi and I shared a look, but said nothing. They were in for a shock when they got the elevator open and three wet, dead ogres tumbled out. Of course, being human, all they would see were oversized men, but still, it was going to be a shock.

The fourth floor was quiet and reeked of ogre, thick and heavy, centering around Mai's door. It overlapped everything else. Again I knew Mai was smarter than the average ogre. Under the layers of ogre scent, I picked out her signature smell, and the blood that was uniquely hers. At her door, I paused, and then knocked softly. "Mai, we lost them."

The door creaked open and there she was. Sweat dripped down her face and she clutched at her middle. "I don't think I'm going to do you much good, Liam. They . . ." She spread her hands so I could see the wound in a quick second before she covered it.

The view of internal organs and intestine was bad, but not insurmountable. "I've seen worse." I stepped in and Levi shut the door behind him, quietly this time. Looked like the kid was learning.

I helped Mai back to her room and laid her on her bed. Around the apartment were signs that there had been a child, and not that long ago. The smell of milk on Mai made more sense now too; the baby hadn't been gone long enough for her milk to entirely leave her.

An empty crib. Blankets folded on a change table. A basket of toys in one corner of the room. I didn't want to think about the possibility of Rylee and me seeing the same emptiness.

I shook my head. "Let me get a better look."

"What, are you a healer now, too?" She panted for air around the words.

"No, but I'm trained for emergencies like this." I put my hands over hers. "Let me see if we can stem some of the bleeding at least."

"You don't understand, they scrambled my guts. They know they'll be able to find me eventually, and I can't heal this. This is a mortal wound." She put her hands over mine. "They know they've got me. This isn't the first time they've hurt me bad. They did something similar when . . . when my boy died. But they had Bly heal me."

I frowned and sat on the edge of the bed. "What are you talking about?"

She drew in a slow breath and grimaced, her lips twisting tightly until they bled of color. "They did this to show me that I have no one left who would stand with me. To show me that I am no longer of the tribe, and that I will be slowly killed and tortured as an outsider."

"The ogre who helped you?" I asked, glancing at Levi and he nodded.

"He'll be dead by now. He was my boy's father. He's been helping me hide out, but this time . . . this time, they'll know he turned on them. They'll send a squad after him."

Fuck. I scrubbed my hands over my face and checked the clock. I had at best thirty-five hours before I was out of time. My mind skittered away from the possibility of not making it, a hard thing to do considering the things around the room that all but rubbed in my face the results if I failed. I could leave Mai and try to find another female but . . . I already knew the truth. Mai was a part of our pack now, to the end. Which left me one path.

"I have a few questions. How long can you survive like this?" I asked.

Mai's eyes closed and her lips trembled. "Maybe six hours. I'll fall asleep in the next two, and then I'll just fade. Even if you could get me healed and away from here, they would follow. They will want to kill you all."

I shook my head. "Why?"

"There is a prophecy. I was to be the one to raise the new leader, or a new nation of ogres. Pic . . . he kept me under his thumb, but I never gave him a child. It wasn't until Tul . . . He was the ogre you met, Levi. He and I . . ."

"You had the child," I finished for her.

"Yes." Her eyes filled with tears.

I could see how it played out, but I said it anyway. "You had the child, and Pic killed him because he was a threat being raised by you. And now he wants you dead because dead, you can't get pregnant with another child."

"Even if I survived, I could not have another child. As I said, this is not the first time this particular injury was inflicted. They scrambled my reproductive organs on purpose. They did this so I can't have more babies."

Holy fucking shit, they truly were monsters.

That was not what I needed, another goddamned deadline and a herd of assholes that wouldn't give up. "Give me ten minutes to think this through." I motioned for Levi to follow me into the other room. "Put a call in to Rylee, then set the phone on the counter, and go sit with Mai."

"You want it on speaker phone?" he asked as his finger hovered over the send button.

"No, I'll be able to hear her fine."

He did as I asked, setting the phone on the granite countertop. He hurried away, back to Mai, and I waited as the phone rang and rang. For a moment, I thought Rylee wouldn't answer. There was only one thing that would keep her from picking up. The babies. On the last ring, she picked up.

"Rylee."

She drew a sharp breath. "Liam, tell me."

"I found a female ogre who will come with me. But she's injured. And the ogres here . . . they are worse than even you realized." I did not tell her about being shot in the head. Or leaping from buildings. That could come later when we were lying in bed together and laughing about the horrors we'd faced on our own and together. "They will follow me if I bring her home to you and the babies. I need to finish them off. I need to make sure they can't come after us."

"How are you going to do that? Ophelia left you there, didn't she?"

I gritted my teeth a moment before answering. "Yes. But there is another Guardian here . . . if I can find him. I think he'll help me."

"Liam, I trust you. Do it. The babies are fighters, you know that. They . . . hurry, and I will keep them alive. It will do none of a fuck bucket of good if you bring her and the ogres follow. We'd lose too many people." Gods, she was fierce in her beliefs and it carried us all.

"I'm going as fast as I can," I said, wishing I could reach through the phone and touch her.

"I know."

"Is Doran there?"

She paused and then the leader of the vampire nation came on. "Did you miss me, Liam, love?"

I rolled my eyes. "Doran, what do you know about a lion Guardian?"

There was a pause along with a sharp intake of breath. "Seriously? He's been missing for about ten years. Why, holy shit, that's who you've got to help you?"

"Maybe. Tell me about him."

"He's an ass like most Guardians, but he's one of the good asses. Kind of like you. But hard to pin down."

In the background, there was a slap, and I grinned, easily seeing Rylee whacking him upside the head. As much as the vampire loved her, she saw him more like a wayward brother, or cousin.

"What else?" I asked.

He grumbled something under his breath that sounded like 'touchy damn Tracker.' And she countered with "that's huntress, now, to you."

Doran came back on. "Look, he's strong and fast

and mean. He's a Guardian, what do you want to know?"

"Does he have anything he was drawn too, a place he might want to go?"

"What the hell, are you going to ask him on a date? I don't know, Liam. I know he was missing, that's about it. That and he had some weird talents, like I said."

"You didn't say that."

"Ah, I meant to. Not that I know what any of them are. Good luck, Wolf." His laughter flowed out of the phone line. What an ass.

Doran, even in the midst of chaos, couldn't seem to help himself from being difficult. I hit the end button, irritation flowing through me.

The phone on the counter went dark. I closed my eyes, thinking. The Guardian I'd released had headed north. Where would a lion go if he was set free? If I could find him . . . I would have someone I could arm against the ogres, someone who was strong enough to stand with me against them, which in turn would give me a better chance of success. Then again, I had an insider source in the other room. Maybe I could do this without involving Lion.

I strode back into the bedroom. "Mai, can you answer some questions?"

The front door burst open and I spun around, both guns raised. An ogre smeared with blood, half his body black-skinned, the other half swirled with purple streaks, fell to his knees. Mai let out a cry. "Tul!"

Great, just what I needed, a second wounded ogre. I held the guns on him. "You sure, Mai?"

"Yes, help him please!" She groaned out the last as she tried to sit up.

I tucked the guns away and went over to him, pointing at her to stay where she was. I slung one of the wounded ogre's arms over my shoulder and picked him up with relative ease. His eyes flicked over me, confusion filling them. "Wolf? I heard they shot you in the head."

"I'm harder to kill than that," I said as I lowered him to the bed next to Mai. She reached over and took his hands. I could see his wounds now. One arm was broken, the bone pushed through, the meat of his side had been cut through as though with massive claws. Claws. I grabbed an edge of the sheet and ripped it into strips, helping to bind up Tul. He worked with me, and within a few minutes, he was bandaged as good as we were going to get him.

"Shit, you ran into the lion, didn't you?" Levi blurted out before I had a chance to ask Tul the same question.

He groaned and looked at me. "How . . . you idiots, you let him out? He'll kill anything he sees. That's why we locked the fucker up in the first place."

Somehow, I doubted Tul here was getting the full story. But like any shitty leader, Pic played on his people's fears that Lion would kill them, without there being any real need to fear him. I chose not to point out that Lion hadn't actually killed Tul.

"Where did you run into him?" I asked. That was

the only thing I needed to know right at the moment. "I need his help."

"He won't help you. I'm surprised he didn't kill you. He's a Guardian, you know." Tul closed his eyes and Mai smoothed a hand over his face as if she could ease his suffering. She would have been a good mom. Through her own pain, she fought to take his away.

"Liam, we can't help you," Mai said. "Our mage is the only one who could heal us at this point, and she's being kept bound up, the same way I was before Tul helped me break free."

That got my attention. "Why didn't you mention that before?"

She grimaced and Tul put a hand on hers. "Because she makes Pic look like a pussy cat. She's meaner than all the men combined," Tul breathed out. "She only had a soft spot for Mai."

I leaned over them, a thought breaking through. "Did she speak the prophecy?"

Mai's eyes flicked to mine and she slowly nodded. "Yes."

"Then we need her, more than just to heal you. She can convince the rest of the ogres, Pic included, to let you go." I ran a hand through my hair. "I'm going to get her first. If I can bring her to you, then you two can be healed."

Tul shook his head. "You'd have to go into the heart of Kerry Park."

"Is it twisted?" I asked, and he nodded even though I didn't even really know what I meant by twisted.

"Bly is deep in the woods, hidden away, and she only comes out once in a while. There is a pool you have to dive to the bottom to gain her attention," he said. His eyelids flickered and he let out a low groan that filled the room. Whatever had been done to him, hadn't just been from Lion. I could see several spots where he'd been shot, the burns on his clothes and the scent of charred skin giving it away.

"Okay," I said. "Then I'll go to the pool and bring her out."

He shook his head. "No, not okay. She hasn't appeared since Mai had the prophecy spoken over her, and anyone who dives to the bottom dies. Do you understand? You can't make it to her, and you can't make it out."

I glanced at Levi, a chill rippling through me. Rylee and her intuition were once again going to save the day. I hoped.

"I think we've got it covered," I said. "We're going to get her, and then bring her to you. Got it? You two just hang on."

Levi helped me get Mai and Tul situated as comfortably as we could and then there was nothing else I could do. There wasn't time to get all the way to North Dakota by vehicle to get Mai and Tul to Doran or Louisa. I had faith the shamans could have healed them, but time was not on our side. Not in the least.

Levi followed me out of the apartment. "Liam, what if I can't?"

"Can't isn't in our vocabulary. Understand?"

He swallowed hard and fell into step beside me. "I'll . . . try."

I lowered my voice. "There is no try, Levi. Do or do not." I winked at him, and he frowned a moment before he caught on.

"All right, Obi-Wan," he said. "There is no try. I'll do it."

It didn't matter to me that he got the reference wrong, or that I could see he wasn't sure at all. The thing was, I knew I was going to ask more of him than anyone probably ever had. And I needed him to know I was with him, and that at least one person believed in him. I'd learned that from Rylee.

Believe, even when you didn't.

And hope to heaven and hell you can pull the win out at the last second.

CHAPTER 8

WE STOOD ON the edge of Kerry Park, staring into the apparently bigger than it looked space. As it was, I could see all the edges from where we were, and even I had to wonder just how big it could possibly be within the wood. Bigger than I wanted, no doubt, if it was even half as twisted with magic as I suspected.

"Levi, I'm going to go in loud. I'm going to draw them to me. Understand?"

"And I'm going to the pool?" He shucked off his jacket and rubbed his hands up and down his arms.

"You've got it in you to make it to the bottom. You can breathe water. You're an elemental." Even if he didn't believe it, I knew it to be the truth. It had to be the truth. "You need to get to Bly, and tell her about Mai. Tell her I know who the babies are that Mai will raise and will lead the ogre nation. Understand?"

He nodded, his young face grim. "And if I run into any ogres?"

"If they don't see you, hide. If they do . . . if they do see you, do what you have to in order to survive. Don't hesitate. No matter what you choose, make your decision quickly."

He swallowed. "I can do that."

I put a hand on his shoulder and gave it a squeeze. "I have faith in you, kid."

He stood a little straighter, the hunch in his back disappearing.

I rolled my shoulders and checked my two guns. I loaded them both. Each held six shots. Twelve shots all together, and I had another eight rounds in my back pocket. Twenty shots and easily a hundred ogres, probably more if I was honest with myself. Which I most certainly was not. Going after Lion wasn't an option when we knew where Bly was, and we had no idea where the rampaging Guardian was. Or if he was even still in the city.

"Count off ten minutes, then head into the forest, stay to the right." That way I'd at least know what direction to keep the ogres moving away from.

"Wait, how do I know I won't just see the park like anyone else? Didn't you say that humans can't see the park for what it really is? What if I'm like that?" Levi asked, and I had to admit, it was a good question.

I narrowed my eyes as I stared at the forest and a shimmering purple aura came into view. My second sight wasn't strong, but the fact that I could see the spell on the park confirmed what I'd already been told. "Squint at the forest. What do you see?"

He squinted and shook his head. "Nothing, just trees."

Well shit, that wasn't going to work then. "I guess we aren't going to get separated after all." Plan A down the drain, moving on to plan B.

I motioned for him to step up and he hurried to

close the few feet between us. "Why don't you think it will work for me?"

"I'm guessing because you are an elemental, because I know that some supernatural spells won't work on them. Something to do with your heritage disrupts the spell for you." Or the fact that he was more human than elemental, but I wasn't going to say that. I needed his belief in himself to be high if we were going to survive the next few hours.

I kept my pace slow, and walked us into the park like I owned the place. The scents that curled around me and up my nose were the kind I expected. Trees, flowers, green things, birds, small mammals, dirt . . . and there at the edges of all those, the growing smell of ogres, weapon oil, leather, and blood. I didn't hurry, I didn't even look around much. "Levi."

"Yeah?"

"When I tell you to drop, you drop."

"Okay."

We kept on walking, getting deeper and deeper into the park. From what we'd seen on the outside, we could have walked through the park four times over. Easily. Yet there was no end in sight, no thinning of the trees, no showing of the blue sky above us. If anything, the trees were getting bigger, the plants more twisted and the birds quieter. I didn't like it, but I knew this was our only chance.

"Levi."

"Yeah?"

"If we get to the pool, anything you can do to get me or you in it, you do it, understand?"

He nodded. "Okay."

So agreeable. Much easier to deal with than Pamela. Though I wasn't knocking her. If I'd had her at my side, not only would Mai and Tul be healed, she would have made sure the ogres never pulled this on anyone again. Unlike Milly, Pamela had a strength to her that would not be denied, and when she decided someone had crossed the line, there was no going back for her. A grin slipped over my lips, thinking of the time I wanted to kill her; when my wolf had seen only the threat of a witch, and not the heart of a girl who would one day rival Rylee for fierceness.

In those quiet moments of musing, my guard dropped, and the ogres took advantage of it. They launched toward us in a single swell like a rising tide that leapt over itself to swallow us whole.

"Drop!" I ordered Levi, praying I could pull this off. This was a Rylee stunt, something I'd have never considered before I met her. Dive in, and come out swinging.

I lifted both guns and squeezed the triggers in a steady staccato that dropped ogre after ogre. They roared as I took them down with a relative ease I knew would come to an end soon enough. Twelve down and I reloaded my last eight rounds. I kept moving, stepping into the trees and leaving Levi behind while I blasted through bodies, drawing them away from the kid and hoping he could find the pool and get the ogre mage to pay attention to him and potentially save six lives. Six. Funny thing, I didn't count my own life in that, only the ogres I was protecting, and Levi.

The empty click of the guns was as loud as the report of a shot gone wild. I tucked the weapons into my waistband, not wanting to drop them even when they were empty. I took off running, drawing the ogres after me. I scented the air, and caught a whiff of spring, mineral-rich water. It was faint, but it was there in the far distance. I bolted toward it. That had to be the pool, it had to be. I urged my wolf to come forward, all but begging the bastard to shift, to help me stand a chance against the ogres. He ignored me again.

"Shithead," I snarled as I dove through a batch of blackberry bushes and landed all tangled on the other side. The vines wove around me, not natural in any sense of the word. Within two heartbeats the thorny vines had dug into my skin, pinning me down and tearing at my clothes. Thirty feet away was a mirrored pool, the surface like glass, it was so still. So close and yet so far. "Bly, Mai is dying!"

I scrambled, fighting to get up, but it was no longer only blackberry vines that tugged at me, but multiple sets of large ogre hands. Ogres that roared with laughter.

"Bly don't listen to intruders. And Mai is already dead, you stupid wolf."

I was yanked up and held tight, stretched as if my limbs were set out on a compass.

"Well, well, looks like we're going to get a double roast." Pic grinned at me. "You're going to pay dearly for killing my men."

A double roast . . . shit . . . they'd snagged Levi too, then.

I was held like that, all four points at the limit of my stretching capability. My back was pressed against a large tree trunk and chains were used to strap my arms and legs behind the tree. None of that bothered me. Until Pic brought out a thick metal collar with a long chain attached to it. A cold sweat broke out on my brow. No, not this again. It took everything I had, every mental reserve left to me not to lose my shit right there and turn into a gibbering mess of howling and snarling wolf.

Pic grabbed my short hair and slammed my head back against the tree trunk so he could slip the collar on. It pinched closed, snagging some of my skin. The pain bothered me far less than the actual collar.

"There we go, chained like the dog you are." Pic slapped my cheek.

"And what about me? You chain up your pussies, too?"

I forced my head to the side. Next to me, on a tree of his own, was Lion. He was cut up, and blood dripped here and there, but even as I watched, his body healed. An ogre was slicing into him over and over again, and his wounds healed as fast as he was injured.

He glared at me. "I could kill you without blinking for putting me in this fucking situation."

I shrugged. "I doubt you'll get the chance. I think they're going to kill me first."

"At least, I will enjoy the show." He snarled and

spit in my general direction. He was collared the same as I was.

I looked down at my own body. The injuries I'd sustained were not healing nearly as fast as his. In fact, I bled freely even from the blackberry wounds.

Was I not a Guardian any longer?

Lion barked a laugh at me and shook his head. "You don't even understand, do you?"

"What, are you a mind reader now?"

Yes, you stupid fuck. It's a talent I have. Just like you, Wolf, have your own talents that apparently you are too fucking stupid to realize.

I blinked several times and Lion nodded. *We can get out of here if we help one another.*

You don't want to kill me now? I raised an eyebrow and he snorted.

Yes, but I'd rather it be you and me against one another, not these odds of a hundred to one.

Fair enough. You got a plan?

Keep their attention on you, one of my chains is weak. I will break it and then set you loose.

Tell me what I don't understand, and what you mean by a talent I should have, I thought.

Lion nodded, his silvery eyes serious. *Done.*

I lifted my chin at Pic. "I've never met an ogre who was unwilling to meet someone on the field of battle. You must truly be the white trash cousin to have to tie your enemies up in order to kill them." The words spilled out of me and Pic slowly turned.

Lion laughed. "Oh, now those are fighting words. This is going to be a pleasure to watch."

Shock coursed through me when the chains were unlocked and I dropped to the ground. The manacles on my legs and arms were heavy, but it was the one on my neck I couldn't help reaching up to touch, digging my fingers under it as if that would somehow get it off me.

Pic grinned, his teeth, sharp, yellowed and broken in places. "You want to fight, Wolf? Then let us see what you are made of. Inside . . . and out."

The ogres around us laughed, howling at me a litany of expletives and curses. But I didn't really hear any of it. I was still too focused on the chain on my neck. My worst nightmare come back to haunt me in the flesh.

The first two ogres rushed me and I dropped to the ground at the last second, letting the one on my left go over my body. I rolled and came up in a crouch.

Guardian is just a word. Lion's voice echoed in my head while I fought. *You are a Guardian by blood, but you switched bodies. I can see it in your mind, that is the obstacle you face. You must convince Wolf that you are still strong enough to carry him even in this new flesh. That your spirit is still your own.*

The second ogre had his back to me, and I yanked a large knife from his belt and drove it into his spine, slicing through the vertebrae. He didn't even stiffen, just slumped and fell forward with a single groan.

I spun and caught another ogre on an upward slash. His arms were over his head as he prepared to slash downward with an oversized axe. I angled the knife in my hand higher. I sliced through his neck, thick black blood spraying in a geyser that arched over me like rain.

"We've got ourselves a scrapper. Drag it out. Make him suffer," Pic instructed, as though telling his boys to add another coat of paint to the house.

Two down, innumerable to go. Even I wasn't that confident to believe I would survive this without help. Where that help was coming from . . . I could only hope Lion held to his end.

Of course I will. I am a Lion, not some ridiculous canine. As I was saying, the Wolf does not trust easily. Your blood was dormant for many years before being woken. When the Wolf finally saw fit, he came forward and you became a Guardian. And now you have another body. Unless you can prove to the Wolf you are still a Guardian, your shifting will not happen.

An ogre with a scar across both eyes snarled at me and swung a length of chain. The metal was spiked, tipped with tiny daggers. The first pass of his flung out weapon drove me back, right into the arms of another ogre. He bit into my shoulder and I snarled, unable to keep the sound in as the bone cracked and flesh tore. Flipping the knife handle around, I drove the blade backward and into the ogre's side three times, feeling organs pop and flesh give before he finally let go. The chain ripped through the air as I was dropped, and I went from the ogre's arms to the embrace of the chain. It wound around my upper body, digging in like tiny fish hooks.

"Oh, this is going to hurt you far more than it will hurt me, Wolf." The ogre snickered and yanked the chain. The hooked blades drove in, cutting into me with the precision of claws as they shredded my body. I was yanked forward and thrown to my knees. The chain was unraveled from me, slowly, as the ogres circled around me. Three, I'd managed to kill three and keep all their attention on me. I couldn't help looking to see if Lion was free.

"Looking for your little boyfriend?" Pic grinned. "Bring him out. Let us show him what we do to tiny humans who interfere."

Oh, this does not bode well for your friend. As I was saying, your talents will display here and there, but you have to be smart enough to recognize them. Which I highly doubt, seeing that you are thick as a brick shithouse in more ways than one.

"Shut the fuck up!" I lunged and hit the ogre nearest to me in the knees. I tackled him while Lion laughed in the background. My wounds and dripping blood made my grip slippery and unstable. I wanted nothing more than to shift, to tear into the ogre, and rip his throat out. To kill them all.

Destroy and maim, to get the chains off me.

My past swept around me and all I could do was think of the ones who'd chained me before. These weren't them . . . but I let the wolf in me unravel any reluctance I may have had left. But I hadn't taken into consideration the chains hanging off each of my limbs. The wolf in me started to come forward, then eased back, shaking his head like I truly was a fool.

You are not the man you once were. The voice was that of my wolf.

I gritted my teeth as a snarl slipped past my lips. I knew it, I couldn't argue with him. This body was not my own. I knew what others saw when they looked at me. Not Liam; they saw Faris with his sharp, dangerous good looks and lean body.

My limbs were grabbed and I was pulled tightly, my thoughts scattering as I was stretched. Like I'd been pulled over a rack. They yanked on me to the point where my joints creaked and my muscles were so tight, I could have been played like a harp.

Levi was dragged into the clearing, held up by his throat before he was tossed into the center of the ring with me. He lay at my feet and stared up at me. "I'm sorry, I couldn't fight them. I tried."

I shook my head but said nothing. Nothing to say now. The only thing to do was figure out how the hell I was getting us out of here and the healer to Mai. One step at a time, though.

"Just what are you two doing here pestering our female, hmm? Looking for the fuck of a lifetime? I just can't quite figure that out." Pic paced between Levi and me. I suspected his curiosity was about the only thing keeping us alive at the moment.

Pic leaned in close to me and lifted one nostril, his face crinkling up. That close, the color of his eyes was clear, like the blue of a raven's wing, so dark, there were colors within the depths. He took a deep enough breath that my hair ruffled toward him.

"You know," he said, "you smell like the woman who was here a week ago."

I held completely still, not wanting to give anything away. But Pic slowly nodded, his eyes lighting up with recognition. "Yes, I can see it now. She comes here, scopes things out and then sends you two in for . . . whatever it is you are looking for. Because even I know it can't possibly be Mai. She's useless now." He grinned at me, showing his teeth in a hard, sharp line. "I made sure of that."

I held his eyes. It was time to throw down my aces. "I think you should call on Bly and ask her about that. I mean, if she's your mage and is all about the prophecies in your tribe, shouldn't you be asking her opinion?"

Pic's face tightened and around him the ogres gave a soft murmuring of assent. I grinned. "See, your men like how I think."

A fist slammed into the back of my head, sending the world into brilliant sparkles that danced around the ogre in front of me. I drew in a breath, held it, and the bright lights slowly faded.

"Do not talk of our mage. She is nothing to a piece of shit dog like you," Pic said as conversationally as if we were discussing the upcoming weather.

Cloudy, with a chance of showers.

I smiled at him. "Really? I heard a story that Bly knows who's going to usurp you on your wee tiny throne. And Mai is going to help them."

Another blow to my head, and then several to my back. Ribs cracked under the fists and feet, the snap of bone echoing through my body, making me jerk against the chains. I coughed, blood flowing from my lungs and into my mouth. I spit to the side, narrowly missing Levi. He scooted back until he was pressed against my legs. Not exactly a safe place at the moment, but he didn't seem inclined to leave me.

His movement drew Pic's attention to him. Shit, that was not going to help matters any.

Slowly, Levi pushed himself up, his whole body shaking as he held his hands out in front of him.

Pic put his hands on his hips and thrust his hips at Levi. "You want to take me on, boy? I'll give you a fucking you'll never forget."

Levi's whole body tensed and then a quiver ran through him as he cupped his hands together.

"Whatever you're going to do, kid, do it now," I said, and all I could do was hope he had some serious bad-ass water magic going on. Because without it, we were going to be in worse shape. If that was even possible.

The thing about thinking like that, though, was that fate was a bit of a jokester, and often liked to show you just how very bad things could get, indeed.

Indeed.

Chapter 9

LEVI SHOOK, AND between his hands the water built up, as though he were making a snowball prior to the freezing of the particles. He never got further than that.

From the left, an arrow shot through the ranks and buried into Levi's side. He cried out, lost his concentration and fell to the ground in a puddle of his own making. I jerked against the chains and dragged the ogres who held the end of them with me as I bent to cover Levi's body. Three more arrows sang through the air and two of them hit me in the back, burrowing deeply into the muscle between broken ribs. The third slammed into the ground right next to my head, narrowly missing my cheek. I could barely draw breath around the two arrows, but there was no way I could move off the kid and open him up to more injury. He was family.

He was part of the pack.

Lion, now would be a good time to break free, seeing as the distraction you needed is at its limit.

Already done. Have fun, Wolf. Pity you have no ability to breathe and hence speak a proper goodbye.

I lifted my head as Lion dropped from his chains and gave me a saucy wave and disappeared around the tree, his dark form blending into the shadows of the foliage.

"Lion," I whispered, gritting my teeth around the biting,

tearing pain as I took a deep breath and roared. "LION."

The ogres swung around and half of them were gone in a flash, chasing down the bastard of a Guardian. Maybe that wasn't a complete win, but that shit wasn't going to offer help and then just fuck off on us. My mind fuzzed over in a haze of blood and wounds as I was pulled from protecting Levi.

Pic gestured to the kid. "Drop him in the pool, let Bly's magic take him."

Levi didn't struggle as an ogre grabbed him by a foot and dragged him across the clearing to the mirrored pool. Maybe this would be good. Levi had water magic, he couldn't drown. Right? Gods, I hoped not. Otherwise, the kid was done and I couldn't save him. Fuck, I couldn't save him.

"I see the hope in your eyes, Wolf. The thing you don't understand about Bly is she loves blood and death more than she gives a shit about even her own kind. He won't survive, no matter what kind of silly, piss-poor magic he can stir up."

"Levi." I said his name and his eyes rolled so he was looking at me. Upside down and being dragged to his death, but looking at me. "Believe." I said the word, but didn't really put any stock into it. Belief was Rylee's realm, not mine. But I'd seen her go through things that would have killed, destroyed, and torn apart anyone else. Belief had been her mantra, from the moment I met her until the moment I thought I'd lost her forever. If it was good enough for her, it could be good enough for us.

Levi's mouth tightened and a tear fell from one eye. I had no idea if that meant he trusted me or was terrified and thought he was going to die. I was betting on a bit of both. Hell, I didn't know how the hell we were going to get out of this. We had no backup coming, Ophelia had left, we were surrounded by a mob of psychotic ogres. There really wasn't much I had left in me to fight them.

Pic made an upward gesture with one hand and I was yanked to a standing position. The arrows dug in farther as if actively seeking internal organs.

The ogres' leader clasped his hands at chest height, like some sort of politician speaking at a rally. "Shall we watch your young friend get destroyed?"

I was turned, and my head held so I had no choice but to see Levi dragged the last few feet to the mirrored pool. I could have closed my eyes, but I wasn't going to be a coward. If this truly was his death, he deserved to have someone witness it. Even if I shortly followed him. I couldn't even drum up the concern with my own death. I'd come so close before; hell, I'd died before and I remembered the process clearly. Levi wasn't tossed into the water. Instead, he was laid at the water's edge like an offering to the old gods. He lay there and nothing happened. I rolled my head to the side and lifted an eyebrow at Pic.

"That, is truly terrifying." Well, shit, I'd officially been with Rylee long enough that her knack for making a situation worse had rubbed off on me. The thought made me smile.

A few ogres snickered and Pic sent a glare out that stilled any mirth.

Then Pic shrugged. "She will come for him when she is ready. I think it's time we take this wolf to task for fucking with us, yes? For crossing into our territory and pissing on what is ours!"

The ogres roared together, the sound like that of a train tearing up a track, its brakes pulled off so it could thunder out of control.

I was dragged backward until I was pinned against a tree once more with Lion right back where he started to one side of me.

"You know, you could have let me get away," he said, without a hint of malice.

I looked at him. "Would you have let me get away?"

A laugh burst out of him, and his chains rattled. "Hell no." He calmed himself, but didn't stop smiling. "You realize we're probably going to die here?"

A sudden and complete certainty rolled over me that I wasn't. I'd faced worse than Pic, hell, I'd faced demons that would have eaten him up like a midnight snack without an effort.

"You might, Lion, but that's because you're an oversized pussy."

The ogres ooohed, but Lion just laughed. "Rich, coming from the martyr of our kind. You, Wolf, have never realized your own strength. You always let yourself die because you think the world needs your death. Did it never occur to you that maybe, just maybe, this world would be better with your life in it?"

His words were sincere and I stared at him, knowing that what I was about to say completely contradicted the situation we were in. But . . . that didn't change the truth. "I don't plan on dying."

Pic laughed. "You might not be planning on it, boys, but I surely am. Time for a little target practice. Have at 'em. No head shots. I want them to see this happen, and I want it to last as long as we can."

The mob whooped in their excitement with only a few groans at the head shot bit. They split into two sets of double lines. The lines in front of Lion went first, giving me a front-row seat at what was about to be dished out to me. An ogre from each line threw weapons of their choice at the Guardian chained to the tree. One hit in the center of his belly with a curved axe, the other missed with a straight-edged knife. They went and pulled their weapons—Lion grunted as the axe was yanked out—and weapons in hand, they went to the back of the line.

Then the next two ogres were up—one with a bow and arrow, the other with a crossbow. I didn't watch any more. I didn't need to. I had my own line that drew my attention with a morbid fascination. Not like I could stop it from happening, so there wasn't as much fear as I'd thought.

I locked eyes with the ogre in the left line. He grinned. "I'm going to eat you when we're done." He drew his arm back and let something fly. It spun through the air, catching the light here and there.

A throwing star thudded into my right thigh. The pain wasn't immediate, so I just stared at the edges that stuck out of me as the blood pooled up around the wound. The bolt from a crossbow slammed into my right shoulder, pinning me to the tree. The ogres hurried forward to retrieve their weapons, making sure to yank them hard. The ogre with the throwing star licked my face. "Ooh, you are going to taste so damn good."

I was no longer sure he was speaking in a purely knife and fork kind of way.

Knives, arrows, axes, bladed and curved weapons of every kind came at me. They hit more often, far more often, than they missed. At the end, they started to throw rocks, the stones digging into the opened wounds on my chest and belly, some stuck in the slow-closing wounds.

"Having fun yet, Wolf?" Lion croaked out. "Are you done being a martyr? Ready to be the Wolf?"

I closed my eyes and did the only thing I could. I brought up Rylee's image behind my closed lids. The thick curtain of dark auburn hair, the eyes that had been tricolored for so long, now a steady green edged in gold. Her smile lighting up her face, the feel of her skin under mine . . . the pain in my body receded as I lost myself in her, as I lost myself in her love, and all I knew that was good and true in my life.

She was the place I belonged. She was the home I'd craved my entire life.

"You know, I hate to agree with the Lion, because he is an ass. But you're being an idiot, grandson. Yeah?"

I blinked, losing the image of Rylee, seeing it

replaced with my grandfather. He strode between the ogres as they took their turns at Lion and me. They didn't look at him, didn't even pause in their practice. As if he wasn't there.

"Griffin, help us," I whispered. He shook his head, his eyes sad.

"I'm not really here. Not in body, just in spirit, yeah?"

That wasn't going to do me much good.

The ogres' laughter flowed around me as the blood ran down my body.

"Pity, he'd make a handsome rug. You sure you want to mess it up? We could just take his head and be done with it," one of the ogres spoke, didn't matter which one.

I had to fight not to physically react to them; the one injury that would end my life, and Lion's to be fair. Decapitation. The rest . . . the rest I was pretty sure I could heal, thanks to the Guardian blood. Of course, that was assuming I'd be alive at the end of this to be able to even think about healing. I didn't know if numerous blows to the heart, or enough blood loss would do me in.

I didn't know if had enough of a Guardian left to me to overcome the odds.

I stared at my grandfather, blinking to try and clear the blood that flowed from a glancing blow to my forehead. We could have been brothers, at least, back when I'd had my body. Not now, though. Now we were night and day, him with his dark hair and eyes, and me with Faris's blond hair and silvery blue eyes.

"See, that's your problem, yeah?" Griffin leaned against my tree and tapped a finger against my shoulder. "You still think of this body you're in as not *yours*. Wolf picks up on that, says, well shit on a prickle bush, I ain't giving my strength to a character who doesn't even believe he's really who he is, yeah?"

I frowned at him, a spark of pain pulling me away from the vision for a moment. I forced it away and focused on him once more. "I don't understand." My words were slurred, pain filled.

"You could break those chains if you really wanted to. Lion can't, he's not meant for that kind of power. He's got other abilities. You're about as strong as any Guardian can be thanks to your connection to me. But you don't believe it, yeah? You don't believe you're a Guardian anymore, so you aren't, yeah?"

"I can't even shift. How can I be a Guardian?" The words dribbled from my mouth along with a wash of blood that trickled over my lips.

"Tie his head up. Let's aim for that windpipe of his. I'm tired of listening to him mumble," Pic yelled.

They used some sort of woven leather to bind my head to the tree so I stared at the underside of the leaves. The twang of a bow and the sharp pierce of an arrow was first, straight through my throat. I garbled as I struggled to breathe around it.

Over and over, they shot me in the neck, and I waited for the heart shot, but it never came. And I finally understood, that even now, this wasn't so much an execution as torture. They were going to push my body to its limits over and over until they grew tired. I kept my teeth clamped shut, the only rebellion I could give as the space I could draw breath through narrowed with each arrow twang and thud into my flesh.

Lion let out a cry and it was cut off mid-sound. I couldn't move, couldn't see if he'd had his head taken. Was I alone? Panic curled up through me as I struggled to breathe.

My grandfather leaned in, his mouth next to my ear. "I'll only say this once, grandson. When the darkness takes you, you might want to listen to the vampire. He's got a truth for you that you need to hear."

I couldn't breathe, my heart hammered in desperation as I fought vainly against the chains, unable to do more than clink them together. The leaves above my head seemed to grow larger, darkening from green to black as they fluttered down and covered my face, stealing away the last of my breath.

"Rylee." Her name was the last silent word on my lips. I was wrong. I wasn't a Guardian. I knew death. I'd seen it before.

And it had come for me a second time.

CHAPTER 10

A LAUGH I KNEW all too well rumbled through the air. I blinked and looked around me. I stood in front of the tree my body was still chained to, head tied back, neck full of at least two quivers of arrows. A sense of unreality flowed over me.

"Pride, it will get you every time." Faris's voice wasn't really his voice. I knew he'd moved on and crossed the Veil, but could still hear him as clear as if he stood next to me.

There was movement on my right side and I spun, and found myself staring at Faris, like a mirror reflection. Blond hair, bright blue eyes, I knew his face almost as well as I knew my own. Hell, I'd been trapped in his body for almost a year now between the time I'd shared it with him and the time since he'd been burned out.

"What do you mean? How the fuck am I being prideful?" I asked, not angry, just confused.

He shook his head with an exaggerated slowness, walked over to the tree where his body, *his* real body, slumped. Blue eyes lifted to mine. "I told you once that you were wrong. That dying for love wasn't the true sacrifice. I would have lived for her, if I could have. But you, you love to throw it all away, like dying shows how much you care." He snorted and patted the top of his head. The slumped one.

My jaw ticked, and, somehow I knew that wherever we were, I had my body back. I could feel it in the movement of the muscles, the way my hands clenched into fists. Small differences, but they were there. And every day they reminded me that I was not in my own body.

"You think I don't want to live?"

Faris laughed and shook his head. "Yes and no. You were a cop for a long time. Trained to take a bullet for someone else, trained to give until it hurt, to sacrifice yourself for the higher good. But there comes a point where you have to know that being a martyr won't work any longer."

I wanted to snap at him that I wasn't a martyr. But he was the second person to use that word and I wondered if it had some merit. The wolf in me rumbled, almost as if he were laughing at me too. Fine then, three people thought I was being a martyr.

I struggled to push the anger down, and I managed. Barely. "I'm listening," I said.

"Well, shit, that's a first." Faris grinned and made a waving motion with his hand as if to encompass all the trees. "You know where you are right now?"

I shook my head. "No. Should I?"

His eyebrows shot up. "Really, you don't even have a suspicion?"

If I was seeing Faris . . . did that mean I was dead? If that was the case, why the hell would he care to give me a lecture. But then, if that was true, where was Alex? And Erik, Blaz, all those we'd lost along the way? Why just Faris?

"You're currently *mostly* dead, Liam. While not fully decapitated, they punched you full of enough arrows to take you right to the brink." He touched one of the arrows, brushing his hand over the brightly colored feathers in the fletch.

"So what, then? You're just here to gloat?" I raised both eyebrows. Griffin had said to listen to the vampire, and I was trying. But Faris made things difficult on a good day, and it hadn't been even close to a good day so far.

He laughed. "I'm not the one who gets to hold her every night, Liam. You are the one who should be gloating."

I took three strides so we were nose to nose. "I thought we were past this, blood sucker."

He shrugged, but there was laughter in his eyes. This was just another one of his damn games. I backed up. "If I die, then I'm stuck here with you, and I will make your afterlife less than pleasant."

"Oh, well, we wouldn't want that then, would we?" He rolled his eyes.

I realized we were talking in circles. And that I was being an ass as much as he was. I closed my eyes and drew in a slow breath. "If you can help me, then help me."

"Ah, well, seeing as I liked my body when it was mine, I think I will help you."

I opened my eyes and he was no longer laughing.

"It's *your* body, Liam. Not mine. Your voice, your power, your soul . . . all of those are what animate it. Not mine. A body is just a shell, does it really matter that it was mine before? That's your problem. You got a second chance, something most people don't get when it comes to life and death. And you can't embrace it because you hated me so much, you pull away from the body?"

Fuck, I hated it when he was right. I didn't have time for this shit, I had to get back. I had to get Mai the help she needed and get her to Rylee.

"Oh no, you don't get to skip out on this conversation. That's the thing about dying—or in your case—almost dying. We can stand here all day and until we hash this out, you're in limbo."

But to admit it to Faris that he was right? Gods, it was like swallowing gravel and then trying to speak around the rocks. "I hated you for so long. Sharing your body was easier than having it to myself; sharing your body meant it wasn't fully mine. I could still pretend I was me and not you."

His eyes lit up and a grin slipped over his lips. "You want to share again?"

I stared at him, knowing a part of Rylee loved him, that he connected with her on a different level than I had. Insecurities I'd been ignoring roared to the front of my brain. On a visceral level, I knew I was being a fool. But apparently Rylee wasn't the only one who couldn't figure out her new life.

My jaw flexed and ticked as I struggled to work through the multitude of thoughts rushing through me.

"Say it, Wolf. Say the words."

I gritted my teeth, holding my mouth against the

traitorous syllables. In a blink, Faris was beside me, whispering the thoughts that chased me out of my dreams.

"What if she's happy she has my body to fuck now? That secretly, she wanted me more all along? That you were always second to my first?" He said the exact things I could not.

I closed my eyes, but I couldn't hide the truth from Faris. He slapped a hand on my shoulder, steadying me as my guts rolled with horror that he said it out loud, the secrets I kept even from myself. Men didn't talk about shit like this. They did not talk emotions and fears.

"Here's the deal, you idiot." He shook me lightly. "She could have lived a life with me, but she wouldn't have remained the vibrant woman she is. You are, no matter what body you are currently residing in, her heart. Even I know that. I might hate it, but it's the truth. And because I love her, I want her to be happy."

I was on my knees, not remembering when I'd gone down. Faris was crouched in front of me. "I find it amusing this has you so torn up," he said.

"Of course, you do, you're a fucking bastard."

He laughed. "I knew both my parents, thank you very much."

I snorted. "Fine, so I'm an insecure idiot. That doesn't help me with my current situation." I waved at the body pinned to the tree.

"Really, I have to spell it out for you?" He quirked an eyebrow. "Here it is. Your wolf is a Guardian. And you . . . are being a pussy."

I burst out laughing. "Are you serious?"

His eyes weren't laughing now. "How many times have you actually let the wolf out, that you've truly let the power rage? Not since I took that collar off you. Since then you've always held back."

That had been . . . not a particularly good time. I put a hand to my neck, feeling the metal as if it were still there. The collar Milly had placed on me had held my wolf in check, and when the collar was removed the wolf roared forward, taking me over completely. I'd killed witches at a rate that had a bounty on my head in no time.

"That's too dangerous. I can't control him," I said, and the wolf in me snarled.

"That's your problem." He tapped me on the chest. "Stop trying to control him, stop trying to make that body," he pointed back to the tree, "yours, as if it isn't already. You treat it as if it isn't and that's your problem. You *are* the wolf. He isn't separate. That body is *yours* now, it isn't mine."

The scene in front of me wavered and I choked, hands going to my neck. I couldn't breathe.

Faris stared at me. "Your decision. You either live for her. Or you die for her. Which is it going to be, Wolf? I'll tell you now, one of them is easier than the other. And one will allow you to live and grant you more time with Rylee, while the other, well, the other will spell your death."

A lesson from Faris was not what I'd been expecting, not in the least, but . . . the truth seared through me. To offer up my life for her was a sacrifice worth giving if it was needed . . . but to throw myself on the sword because I was insecure in my life . . . that was a different thing altogether.

"Fight for her, Wolf." His words came from far away. "Fight for her."

My whole body spasmed against the chains and I struggled to breathe around the multitude of arrows. No, the arrows didn't belong there . . . I thought about how my flesh should have been healing. I was a Guardian. I was *not* going to die like this.

The arrows slowly, inexorably, pushed out of my skin, plunking one at a time, falling to the ground, sticking in my clothes, but falling. Each removal gave me room to breathe, gave my heart a reason to beat. The last arrow fell and a few slow tears leaked from my eyes streaking down my cheeks. My eyes, not Faris's.

"So, Wolf, you decided to join us?" Lion said. I couldn't see him. My head was still strapped to the tree, so I stared at the underside of the leaves, watching a few fall toward me. There was no sound of ogres, no shuffle of feet or weapons.

"They're gone, if you're wondering." Lion grunted. "Though I doubt that bodes well in our favor. They were still talking about a barbeque as they wandered away."

I ignored him, focusing on my body, listening to the pain, feeling the wounds heal over, my skin sealing up faster than it had before. Faster, because I now knew my purpose. I was a Guardian, not only of Rylee and our pack, not only of the triplets, but if I truly listened to the words of my soul, I was a Guardian of the world.

With that acknowledgement, strength rushed through me, my muscles filled with it, and I snapped my head forward, breaking the leather straps as though they were made of tissue paper.

Lion let out a low laugh. "I think I might stick around to see this after all."

I turned my head to see him still chained to his tree. "Doesn't look like you have much choice but to stick around." My voice was raspy, torn up by the arrows . . . but it was mine. I wiggled my fingers, twisting them to wrap around the chains. Chains, just like leather straps, could be broken. I grabbed hold tightly and pulled with all I had. The metal screeched, giving slowly with a cry like a wounded animal. The links popped and gave, and the tree groaned as the metal bit into the flesh of the bark.

"Fuck," Lion breathed. "I'd heard stories but . . . I wasn't sure."

I relaxed, but was still attached to the tree. Panic clawed at me for a moment before I slowed it. I wiggled one arm, and the chains fell, coming unstuck from where they'd been forced into the tree bark. I worked the chains off my legs, not really thinking about what I'd done, just knowing it had to be this way. Several of the links had come undone, the metal stretched to its brink before letting loose, but still holding. I shook my head and stared at the chains still hanging from my arms and legs.

"Yeah, that's the shitty part." Lion laughed. "You want to let me down now?"

"No." I walked away from him, limping a little as my bones knitted. I went straight to where Levi lay next to the pool. I crouched beside him. His chest didn't move, but I could hear that slow and irregular heartbeat before I even put a hand to his neck.

I rolled him over to see where the arrow had entered.

"You can't save him," Lion said. "But you can save me."

"Shut up." I didn't look over my shoulder at Lion. I kept my attention on the kid. Other than the arrow, he'd not taken any wounds. And while it was bad, it didn't look like it pierced anything vital. I carefully removed it and took a sniff of the tip, immediately recoiling. Poison of some sort, by the acrid smell that burned the inside of my nose. They must have only tipped the one in it because I'd felt nothing like that go through my system.

I threw the bloodied arrow into the mirrored water where it was swallowed up in a single, splash-less gulp. The arrow fell to the bottom of the pool and a pair of eyes blinked up at me. Eyes. Ogre eyes. I stared back.

"Bly."

The eyes blinked once, but she otherwise didn't move. Bubbles raced up from her, as if she tried to speak. As if . . . she were trapped too. I thought Mai had been exaggerating that Bly was bound. Was it possible that the mage could have been tricked? Or was she just hiding out?

I lifted Levi so he was sitting up, leaning against my side. I smacked his face lightly. "Levi, I need you to wake up. Come on, kid."

He didn't stir. I scooped a handful of water and splashed it in his face. He gasped and opened his eyes. "What happened?"

"You've been shot, but, kid, I need you to lift all this water out of the pool." I pointed with my free hand to the mirrored pool.

Levi looked. "I'm not that strong. You saw me, I couldn't even throw water at them when they were taking us both." He shook his head, tears trickling down his face.

"I saw you in the apartment building. You've got it in you to be strong enough. You *are* strong enough, Levi. I know this is new to you, but blood runs true. You are an elemental, just as I am a Guardian." I pointed at the water again. "So lift that water and help me save the triplets, help me save Mai."

He frowned and slowly nodded. With a trembling hand, he reached out and slid it into the water. He closed his eyes and the water rippled around him. Sweat poured down his face as though he were standing under a waterfall. The water bubbled and began to flow out of the borders of the pool, leaving like a thousand tiny rivers that rushed along the ground. At first, just in dribs and drabs, like a slow leak from a rusted-out pipe, and then faster. Faster and faster until the pool and whatever filled it could not keep up with him as he removed the liquid and the area around it looked like a spider web with all the veins of water running from it.

"Well, well, I told them a Wolf would save us all. Those fuckers are idiots. I should have castrated them all and not just Pic," Bly said, her voice raspy with age and something else. Like she'd had a tracheotomy at some point. Though the scar on her neck said knife fight, not surgery.

I stared into the bottom of the now mostly dry pool. The ogre who stared up at me had long gray hair braided to either side, and her back was hunched as though she'd been bent in half and left that way for years. Her eyes, though, were all I really took notice of. Pic was dangerous. This ogre . . . this ogre was the one who would haunt my nightmares. And all she'd done was look at me. I could see through her. I could see her soul and the violence there, the blood of her past, the kills of her past. The glory she'd taken in death. And I needed her help. This had all the markers for an epic catastrophe.

I flipped one of the chains still attached to me down to her. "I'll pull you up."

She grasped the chain, and a shiver of power ran through the metal to me. She laughed, high and tinkling like the notes of a wind chime. Not what I expected at all.

"Oh, Wolf." That was all she said as she gripped the chain. I backed up, pulling her out of the empty pool while a part of me said to leave her there and cover her with water. We needed her help to save

Mai, but I wondered just what we were loosing on the world.

I put a hand on Levi and dragged him back with me as well. Call me cautious, but I didn't want to leave the kid closer to her than I had to.

Once out of the pool she waved at Levi. "Let the water go, Elemental. The spell was broken when the pool was emptied, that was the curse."

Levi opened his eyes and the water fell from where he'd been holding it over our heads. A wash of warm, mineral water smoothed away some of the blood and dirt off me. I didn't take my eyes from Bly, though, not even to blink the water away.

I didn't dare.

"Mai is hurt. She's dying and needs your healing," I said, getting right to the point.

"Ah, little Mai. She's integral to our species surviving." Bly nodded. "But I think Pic is going to make her suffer first, if he hasn't already."

She hadn't let go of the chain yet so I tugged her forward. "Then I will take you to her; you can heal her."

She shook one finger at me. "No, you won't. You will bring me something first. Something I have wanted for a very long time, and no one has been able to gather for me, an ingredient like no other. But you, Wolf, I think you could get it for me."

Anger snapped through me. I looked at the sky above, seeing the way the light was fading. Fading on the second day. We were running out of time; the babies were running out of time.

"I don't have time to find you some godforsaken missing flower petal, or root of a plant that no longer exists. Lives are on the line, and I won't waste time with some wild goose shit chase."

She clapped her hands together, that high tinkling laughter spilling out of her again. "No, not that kind of ingredient, Wolf. I need you to bring me the head of Pic. That is what I require. It will work in your favor too. But his death must come, before Mai's life."

I took three steps and had a hand around her throat before I thought better of it. I lifted her off the ground so we were eye level. "And if I don't agree?"

Her eyes glittered, and I squeezed harder, feeling the bone of her neck creak and not giving a shit that another ounce of pressure and I would snap her neck. She was not on our side, not by a long shot. But I needed her. That was the only reason I set her down. I snarled at her. "Swear to me that you will save Mai's life if I bring you Pic's head. Swear it."

She smiled, showing off several oddly spaced sharp teeth. "I swear it on the breath of my grandson Tul that I will save Mai no matter the cost if you bring me Pic's head."

I held my hands out to her. "You can remove these chains?"

She snorted, snapped her fingers and the chains fell from both me, and from the sounds of it, Lion behind me.

"Levi—" I pointed at him, intending for her to heal him up as well.

Bly made a waving motion with one hand and Levi

was dragged by seemingly nothing across the ground to her feet. "No, the young elemental stays with me. For insurance. I will stem the poison in his veins, but I will not cure him until you bring me what I want."

I was in her face in a split second. "He'd best be alive when I get back, or you will see that your past holds nothing to what I will do to you."

She arched one eyebrow. "Wolf, we have met before, so I will say this. Of all the deaths I've faced, I'd welcome the one you bring. But not today. Today you have a chance to make things right, not only for your life, but for an entire species. Pic must die if ogres are to flourish again. There is no other way. I may be death's whore, but I want my people to live."

I spun on my heel, scenting the air, knowing in my gut she would hold to her word. Lion fell into step beside me. "I'm coming with you."

"Fuck off. You'll probably tell them where I am," I said.

"You don't understand. I . . . " Lion put a hand on my arm, stopping me. "We are some of the last Guardians, Wolf. You and I, a few others scattered around the world. I have lost that fire to care for others. I need to find it. As good a place as any is a full-out battle." He let go of me and shifted into his lion form.

I didn't think about what I had to do and what it would take. I let the instincts carry me forward.

I didn't ask my wolf to shift, I didn't demand anything. I thought of being a wolf, my spirit and body melded and reformed into the wolf I knew I was no matter what flesh held my soul. Black from tip to tail, I stood in the same body as I had every time I'd shifted before.

Except when I looked down, my right paw was a pale blond, not unlike the color of my hair when I was human. My hair, not Faris's.

Now you're getting it. Faris's voice whispered over my senses, and I turned to look over my shoulder. He stood there, leaning against a tree, behind Bly. He lifted a hand. "Live, Wolf. For both of us. And give her a kiss from me."

I tipped my head back and a howl roared from my belly, from every fiber of my being. The call of the hunt. The call to track down and destroy my enemies, the ones who would keep me from protecting those I loved. The call to hunt those who scarred the world, the ones who would break bonds and vows.

The sound of the howl sent the birds into flight, and the small mammals under the brush fled.

Bly waved both hands at us. "Go on now, I doubt Pic is going to just wait for you. He'll have some ace up his sleeve to throw. In other words, hurry the fuck up."

I drew in a breath, my nose a thousand times more keen in this form. I found Pic's scent easily, a musty maggot-ridden stink that tasted of madness and blood on the back of my throat. With two strides, I took off, leaping through the forest, my paws hitting the ground silently. Lion stayed close to my side, a blur of gold and black.

No thoughts passed between us. Nothing but

the rush of trees, of wind and the wild, of my blood pounding, freedom and power blending under my skin, building into a strength I'd never understood before. The wolf that had been separate from me for so long, finally, fully melded into me, content with what I now understood. I was strong enough to accomplish my goal and get back to my mate, whole, where I'd previously been broken.

Lion let out a roar that rattled the earth, and I echoed it in a howl that blended with the sounds of his snarls, like a two-piece orchestra built on the swelling wildness within us. As Guardians we were designed for only a few things: To protect the world from the ones who would harm it. Ones like Pic. To keep the world, and not just those we loved, safe. To demand justice and inflict it like the executioners we were created to be.

The wind caught through my fur, like feeling Rylee was there with me, urging me on, her voice in my ear telling me she trusted me. Her hands silken, the beat of her heart in time with mine, even with the distance between us. She was there, and for a moment, I glanced to one side, expecting to see her, the sensation was so strong.

She wasn't, but there were others creeping in with us. The ones who this forest had created a shelter and a prison for. Smaller wolves, foxes, and an oversized badger streaked along with us, slipping in from the shadows. Captured, I saw in them the destruction the ogres had wreaked on their lives. Caged within this forest to give the ogres prey to hunt close to the city.

Another howl ripped out of my chest, sorrow for them, and a promise to take their vengeance and make it justice. The cacophony of howls, snarls and roars lit up the air, blasting through the forest and making the magic around us shimmer under the strength of so many hearts.

Lion let out a monstrous roar, the call of the king to his kind. The cats came, cougars, four of them streaking in low to the ground, their long lean bodies leaping in tandem with Lion's. A paler gold, they flanked him, going with him into the battle that waited.

The wolves and foxes swept in close to me, their eyes bright with the thrill of the hunt. Of being a part of a pack that would take out an enemy threatening them all.

Pack leader.

Alpha.

Guardian.

Wolf.

Liam.

Power rippled out around us, calling those who'd been wronged. A werewolf, old and gray around the muzzle, joined the fray, and other shifters of every kind. Captured and tortured within the forest. Some were missing limbs, some were missing eyes, some could barely stand. Yet they came, and their hearts were strong, even if their bodies were weak.

The howl that coursed out of me was one born of emotion, seeing their strength where mine had nearly failed. They were with us, for no matter what this leap of faith held, it was better than being left to rot in a forest that would keep their deaths drawn out.

The forest began to thin, but I did not slow. Pic's scent was still ahead of us and growing stronger. We burst out of the trees and into the street. Traffic slammed on brakes as we leapt across the hoods of cars, landing in the middle of the road, as if the zoo had spilled over the edges. There was no other way but straight to Pic. The ogres were there, getting into vehicles. Some turned, a few saw us, but they stood stunned as we came for them, as we came for their blood and their lives.

Lion and his bevy of cats struck first, their claws taking ogres out at the legs, dragging them down and ripping bellies open wide. Lightning-quick as only cats could be, they blasted through the first ranks of the ogres.

Cars backed away, sirens sounded at a distance, and I knew the cops would be on us in no time with their weapons that worked around the supernatural. I couldn't let that happen. I motioned with my muzzle at the ogres and the wolves and foxes shot into the fray. They took the ogres down, two wolves, or a wolf and a fox to each ogre. Dragging them from the rest, separating them from the mob. We had to make this fast, we had to end it now.

Three ogres came in from the right, weapons swinging. I leapt without thought, taking the center ogre down, tearing his throat out as we fell. We barely touched the ground when I'd spun and buried my teeth into the leg of the next ogre, pulling him off his feet. He went down with a thud, his head cracking on the pavement. The old werewolf was on him in a flash, tearing his throat out with a speed and viciousness that spoke of years of pent-up rage. I didn't watch, but spun and took the next ogre from behind. I jumped up, my paws on either side of his neck and snapped my jaws over his spine. I pulled with all I had, removing his head with an ease that even surprised me.

Around us, the world was a medley of chaos that erupted with the shrieks of terrified yet still-watching humans, along with the cries of the ogres as they went down, and with them both the growing sirens of the police cars in the distance.

I didn't want to shift into my human form. I'd missed being able to run on all fours more than I'd realized. But I had to shift in order to keep those who fought at my side safe.

I slid back easily, thanking the gods that I'd learned how to shift and keep my clothes intact so I didn't end up baring my ass to the world. Of course, Faris would have had no compunction about going nude. I could hear his laugh on the wind with those thoughts rolling through me.

"Old man." I glanced down at the werewolf, and he shifted with me. Like most werewolves, this meant he was completely naked. I slapped a hand on his shoulder. "We've got to stop the cops. Those weapons they have can't become a part of this or we will be done in."

He gave me a nod, gray head bobbing and eyes bright with eagerness. "You've got a plan?"

I nodded. "Take one of those cars and drive right into them. Think bumper cars."

"That won't stop all of them," he pointed out.

"No, it won't. But they love a good car chase, too."

All I could do was hope it would take some of them out of the battle.

A roar went up from the ogres and I spun to see the wolves being scattered left and right by a club-swinging monster.

Pic.

"Go." I shoved the old man, getting him moving, and he ran toward the abandoned cars in the middle of the street. I didn't watch to see that he'd done what I asked. The animals were still taking the ogres down, but it seemed for every ogre killed, two more stepped up in his place. It *was* like an anthill, with a never-ending run of monstrous black ants that couldn't be stemmed. Time to cut the head off the one who started the anthill. Kill the king, end the battle. No matter how it ended, I would end it now one way or another.

"Pic, you piece of shit, let's finish this. You and me, one fight and we can spare the rest of their lives."

He laughed at me. "You think you can challenge me? No, that is for ogres only. And you are not an ogre. I will fight you, though. But not before I do this."

He held out a hand and an ogre shot forward, putting a tiny rolling globe into it. I froze, recognizing the potential, if not the exact spell. I'd seen enough of Pamela and Milly's spell bombs to know we were in serious trouble. Flames licked out around the rolling ball. This was going to hurt.

CHAPTER 11

I WAS WRONG ABOUT Pic, though. I should have listened to Bly. Should have recognized that he would have a way out of this mess, a way to keep my attention away from him. He rolled the glowing orb from one hand to the other, miniature flames lighting it up.

"Your little friend is still in there, isn't he? Did you know I put Mai and her boyfriend in the forest, too? That's what we were doing. I knew you would come out, and we stuffed them in as you left the pool." Pic swung and threw the spell at the trees at the edge of the park. The flames shot up instantly. The first row of trees burned so quickly and hot, they exploded, sap ripping from them in a spray of burning hot liquid.

Laughing, he turned away, snapping his fingers. "Kill those you can, the rest, we'll gather them up later."

Horror flowed through me. Without Pic's head, Bly would not heal Mai.

Mai and Levi were in that inferno.

The triplets would die without Mai's help.

I shifted and leapt . . . right at Pic. I knocked him down, teeth snapping at the back of his neck. He rolled, a short sword in one hand as he turned and tried to slide the weapon across my throat. He caught my shoulder and drove the blade to the bone. "You stupid wolf, you don't know when to quit."

My back feet scrabbled against his legs, digging in gouge marks as I fought to stay on top of him. My front claws dug into his leathery hide, but there was no real purchase for me. Which only left my teeth. I grabbed his right pec in my mouth and bit through the muscle, tearing and ripping. He kept his hands up, screaming at me as he drove his weapon into me over and over. The pain blinded me, but I followed my nose as I tore through his chest. Ribs suddenly appeared through the blood, white and no different than any other skeleton. He screamed for help, perhaps suddenly realizing that his death hovered close.

Around me, I felt the animals shift, creating a circle of protection. They gave their lives as I fought to take Pic's. Their cries were defiant, a last howl or snarl to the world that they would not be caged, they would not be taken again. That they would rather die free than live caged.

I had my right paw digging at the ribs, the blond fur pure red with blood. Ribs gave way to a beating heart and I drove my muzzle through the tight space. The heart beat frantically, and I closed my mouth around it, squeezing it like an overripe tomato. It burst in my mouth, life blood flowing down my throat, burning a path to my belly like over-proofed whiskey.

Below me, Pic gave one final kick and then stilled, his arm falling to the side. His sword was still jammed in my side, but as my body healed, it pushed the blade out. I raised my head and howled, the sound guttural and wet with the life I'd taken. The ogres went silent, they stopped their fight. The animals left around me were tense, waiting. I stood, wobbling. I shifted into my human form and stared at the ogres in a slow turn. "Leave now and you might survive this day."

They scattered like leaves on the wind, spineless without their leader. I took Pic's sword, grabbed his hair, and sliced through his neck. His face was slack with only a glimmer of surprise etched in it. A wave of heat pressed against my back. Lion approached me and shook his mane as he shifted. He was coated in blood, his skin slick and shiny with it.

"The flames have eaten most of the park, and with that the magic is failing. If you go in, you'll be as trapped as those you are trying to save."

I shifted to my wolf form and grabbed Pic's head with my mouth. I didn't know if Lion was right, but I was guessing he was on to something. It didn't matter, though. There was no turning back. I had to get Mai and Levi out of there. I wasn't going to die. I was going to live, no matter what it took.

I raced toward the burning trees, the smell of wood and seared fur filling the air as I launched into the heat.

The flames licked at me, alive in their desire to consume anything they could. My fur crisped, and the pads of my paws blistered as I ran. I squinted against the smoke and held my breath as long as I could. I knew only the direction I had to go in order to get to the pool. Lion was right, around me the magic was fading and Kerry Park was being sent back to the form the humans knew. Within the flames, I could see the purple swirls of the magic that had made the park larger than it was supposed to be, and could see them breaking down in front of me.

I put everything I had into moving faster, of getting ahead of the unraveling of a world I needed to hold together a little longer. Just a little longer was all I asked, long enough to get my people and get the hell out.

I drew in a breath, forced to by a pair of screaming lungs and muscles that began to cramp in protest at the lack of oxygen. Not that the breath helped much in that department. Smoke filled my nose and I coughed, stumbled, fell into the flames, got up, and ran again. I flattened myself to keep my head as near to the ground as I could while still holding Pic's stupid head. I could almost hear him laugh at me, a final bomb thrown to show his contempt for all those around him.

The flames thinned, as suddenly as if water had been thrown on them, and I fell into the clearing where the smell of my and Lion's blood permeated the air. I was on my side, panting, finally able to take stock of injuries that were not healing as they should have been. For a moment, I thought it was because of my doubt . . .

"Ah, the magic burns deeply." Bly bent over me and I cringed back, not wanting her to touch me. I didn't dare shift, uncertain I could even hold my body together when I was so badly burned.

The wind whipped around us, and the flames bent

in our direction. Bly grinned. "Your boy can only hold the flames so long, despite the blood in his veins." She motioned to Levi. He was on his knees, his hands outstretched, and it was only then I saw the wall of water I'd fallen through at the very edge of the clearing. That moment of crispness that had cooled the flames and kept me from burning up as I lost my footing.

Bly kicked at Pic's head. "Doesn't much look like Pic, all burned up as it is. How do I know you didn't just go and kill any old ogre and bring his head to me?"

I lunged at her, snarling, my paws blistered so badly that even a step left me sticking to the ground. Behind her came a soft cry.

"Bly, please. Please help us. For your grandson's sake. For the sake of our people," Mai said.

I saw her, and limped to her side. My skin was cracked and bleeding, open from the blisters that broke out everywhere the fire had touched me. Magic bit deeply when it finally took hold, I knew that, and this was to the bone in several places. I lay beside Mai. I thumped my tail once, twice, and then let it still. I'd done all I could. Now it was up to Mai to make Bly see what she needed to do. What she'd promised to do.

Tul lay next to Bly, his eyes closed, his chest barely lifting. His death was coming, I could smell it on him, the slow breakdown of organs and muscles as the tissue died. But Mai didn't know that.

Bly hobbled over, taking her sweet as time as Levi groaned under the strain of holding the flames back.

Rylee had been right about him. Not that I was terribly surprised. She was so often right about the wayward souls she brought home.

Without him, we wouldn't have made it this far. If we survived, I needed to be sure to tell him that.

I watched as Bly went to her knees and cupped her hands around Mai's face. "I told you that you would raise the child that would save our people."

"Yes," Mai whispered, pain lacing her voice.

"But you are barren."

Mai's eyes flicked to me. "There is more than one way to raise a child. They do not have to be of my blood to be mine."

Yes, she was the right one. I could see her now in our lives easily, filling a space I didn't think even Rylee knew was truly empty. The space that Dox and the ogres she'd called friends had left empty with their deaths.

Mai was pack, and that was why I'd been drawn to her, why I'd found her so easily.

Because she belonged with us.

Bly nodded. "Then let this be done. As I swore on the last breath of my grandson, I will heal you."

She put one hand on Tul and other over Mai's heart. Mai cried out, "No, don't, don't, please!"

Don't what?

Oh, shit.

Tul's breathing slowed as Mai's heartbeat grew stronger. The wounds in her belly closed over and as she gained strength she tried to fight off Bly's hand. But it was as if the old ogre mage was made of steel, and Mai was a child beating at a door she could not open. As suddenly as she'd put her hands on Mai and Tul, Bly stepped back.

"It is done. I've had enough with all of you." There was an edge of tears to her voice, but it was gone in a flash, making me doubt I'd even seen it.

She snapped her fingers and a slice in the air opened . . . a cut in the Veil. I stood, cracked and bleeding as wounds reopened and oozed with pain and pus. We had to get through there, it was our way out of the forest. No matter where Bly was going, it would allow us a chance to get out of the fire and away from the remainder of the ogres. Who I had no doubt, once they regrouped, would be on our asses like white on rice.

Bly stepped through the slice in the air and shut the Veil with a snap, and without even a glance behind.

I sagged, my head drooping. Mai cradled Tul to her chest, sobbing as though her heart was gone. As though she would not leave him. Wounded, I needed help from my own pack. What I wouldn't give to see one of my own stride through the forest.

Levi . . . still had his cell phone.

I forced my body to shift to human. I lay on my back, my clothes seared to me in places and the wounds even more apparent now that they weren't hidden by the thick fur of my body. "Levi. The cell phone . . . Call Rylee."

"I can't do that and still hold the water." He panted the words.

I crawled to him and dragged him back so we were

all at the edge of the pool. "You can't hold it forever. Let it go, call Rylee."

His eyes were filled with fear and the flickering image of the flames. I gave him a nod. "Trust me. We're all getting out of here." Gods, I hoped I was right.

He dropped his hands, the water fell to the ground creating a thin moat, and the flames raged, the sound of the fire eating the magic and trees filled the air. He fumbled to get the phone out. "There's only four percent left on it."

"Call."

I stared at the flames, listening as the phone rang through. Rylee picked it up, I heard the sound of her breath, the hitch in her voice. "Liam."

"I need help."

"Pamela and Marco are—"

The phone went dead. I pushed Mai and Levi into the water of the pool. "Stay." I shifted, my body feeling as if it were breaking as my skin tore. I tipped my head back, thinking of Pamela. She was part of my pack, a little sister, a wolf cub with a bite that could defy even the biggest wolf. I howled, putting my power and strength into the howl, calling her. Calling her to me.

The sound rippled out of me, through the trees. Once, twice, three times I called and then the smoke slammed into me, like a wall of bricks crushing my chest. Someone grabbed my back legs and tugged me into the pool. Mai held my wolf body so I floated in the water with her.

"You did all you can," she said. "I'm glad you

came. You stopped Pic. That . . . that is worth our lives."

No, I was not going to die. I tipped my head back again and howled, begging for Pamela to hear me. Begging her to find us.

The flames surrounded us at the edge of the pool and the water began to heat. I knew we would be boiled alive. But I didn't close my eyes. I stared into the fiery canopy above us as the leaves fell in flames and bits of branches and bark exploded into the air. Because above us, that was where Pamela would come.

I had to believe.

Belief was all I had left, and I refused to let it go. The water heated and I howled . . . this was the last. I would not have any more strength. I could feel it slipping. I suspected that being burned alive could potentially end my life as a Guardian if it was bad enough, but at that moment I wouldn't even consider that possibility.

A shadow passed over us, the wings of a gray Harpy I knew all too well. I howled Pamela's name as I shifted and the trees were blown back around us and the earth heaved. Mai screamed and Levi clung to me, his fingers biting into the blistered wounds. But I couldn't be happier. The fear was gone. My throat was blistered down the length inside, which made talking nearly impossible. I stumbled out of the water and went to my knees. I was a Guardian, toughest of the tough, but I still needed my pack around me.

Pamela and Marco landed and she flicked her

fingers at the flames. They went out in a snap, as though she'd stolen the air from them. Her hands raised above her head, the glow of green and blue in her fingertips grew until it seemed to be uncontainable. She let the magic go and a blast sped outward, a spray of water and earth that damped the last of the flames. Wisps of smoke curled up here and there, the blackened char of the forest right to the edge of the pool, a testament to how very close things had come.

Her blonde hair spun as she turned to me. "Liam!"

She ran to me and caught my face in her hands. I flinched but held still. Her magic spilled over me, healing the wounds and wiping away all trace of the magical flames that had eaten at me.

"I have never been so glad to see you in my life." I wrapped her in a hug and spun her around, laughing. She patted me on the back.

"I missed you, too." I felt the hiccup from her, like a tiny sob. I put her down and held her at arm's length. There was a deep sorrow in her that hadn't been there before she left on her last trip. But now was not the time to ask. "You got it in you for one more healing?"

She nodded and I took her to Levi. His eyes widened as he took her in. I knew what he saw. A beautiful girl with long silken fair hair and summer blue eyes. However though she was physically young she didn't act it, and her eyes told a different story than her age. One of sorrow and strength, of fear, doubt and understanding that she was more than she seemed.

She took his face in her hands and he shivered as her magic ran over him. I held a hand out to Mai and helped her out of the pool. "Pamela, we have to get Mai back to the babies."

Pamela drooped. "Liam . . . "

I held up a hand, stopping her. "No, don't tell me it's too late." No, we couldn't be too late. Not for the babies. We couldn't have gone through all this, all this death and destruction only to fail at the finish line.

"There has to be a faster way to get home," I said.

Mai shook her head. "Bly . . . she could have stayed and helped us jump the Veil."

I closed my eyes, refusing to look at Pamela. I would not ask that of her, and besides that, I wasn't sure she even knew how. "How long have we got left?"

"Hours," Pamela breathed. "They have hours, at best."

I did a quick spin around, seeing some of the animals who'd fought at my side creeping back in. But it was Lion I pointed at. "We need a way to cross the Veil. Now."

He put a splayed hand to his chest. "Why the hell are you pointing at me?"

"Because I think that's how you came to Seattle from wherever you're from. You jumped the Veil using an entrance," I said.

He shook his head, then sighed and nodded. "It's at the top of the Space Needle. Which is currently closed to the public. And I don't mean with yellow tape and an overweight, old security guard we can offer a donut to so we can slip by."

I leaned back, remembering Lion running away in

the zoo rather than try and take us out as everyone said he should have. "Couldn't get in the other night, could you?"

He shook his head. "No. It was guarded with ogres as well as cops. I think it's their out, escape plan B if you will."

Mai nodded slowly. "I remember Pic talking about an exit strategy. I bet that was it."

The *it* being a doorway through the Veil. I was betting it would take us to the castle, a center point in the Veil that led to a multitude of places. Including the North Dakota badlands which were a short distance from home. Or at least, I was hoping the cut in the Veil would bring us to the castle. Taking the doorway, wherever it led, was our only chance, a gamble I was willing to throw all my chips on.

"Priority number one is getting Mai to Rylee," I said.

Pamela nodded. "Marco, how many of us can you carry that short distance?"

Marco looked over us. "All but one, I think. Two on my back, two in my claws is going to max me out."

Lion shrugged. "I'll meet you at the Space Needle. I can go on foot and make it in no time."

I nodded. "I'll go with Lion. We'll meet the rest of you at the base of the Needle. Don't stop for anything, Pam."

She gave me a grin, a flash of humor on her lips. "I never do. I did learn from Rylee, remember?"

I snorted as I shifted into my wolf, Lion following me a split second later. I motioned for him to lead, seeing as he knew exactly where we were going. Marco lifted off as we leapt forward, Mai and Pamela on his back, and Levi held tightly in the clutches of one talon. The last thing I saw was Levi clinging to Marco, the kid's eyes clamped shut. I wanted to tell him to take in the view, but then I recalled the flight on Ophelia. Perhaps it was best he just kept his head down.

Lion and I raced through the streets of Seattle with more than one car hitting the brakes as we ducked and dived between them. There was only so much of the supernatural the humans could deny. A wolf the size of a small pony and a lion running down the center line of traffic? Yeah, too much for even the biggest disbelievers.

The Space Needle was easy to see once I looked for it. Even without Lion, I'd have found my way to it as it rose above the city, easily recognizable. As we approached, I tensed, fully expecting the place to be crawling with ogres as they made a run from the disaster of their tribe.

There were yellow tape lines and a few police officers, but no ogres, neither in sight or in scent. I glanced at Lion, but he just shrugged as we slowed and shifted between one stride and the next into human form. "Maybe they figure they can't leave without Pic?"

That didn't make any sense. I frowned and looked up at the sky as Marco dropped from the top of the Needle in a straight dive. He swept his wings outward at the last second, stopping the headlong rush. Mai and Pamela jumped off his back, and Marco released Levi. The kid stumbled, his face green and his knees weak. Pamela steadied him with a hand. I saw the bright flush on his face as he pulled away from her.

Helped by a girl . . . he was going to have to get used to that. The reality in our lives was that the women were powerhouses in their own right.

And as liable to pull our asses out of the fire as we were to save them. Strike that, Rylee had saved me far more times than I'd saved her. I shook my head and strode toward the main entrance.

A guard stepped up, a city cop with him.

"Move," I said, the word growling from my lips. The guard moved back, but the cop went for his gun. I was on him in a flash. I snapped his arm and took both weapons. The guard beside him stuttered, went white, and fell backward in a dead faint. I motioned for the others to go through the doors.

I paused and looked back at the male Harpy. "Marco . . ."

"No worries, Liam. I'll meet you at home." He bobbed his head once and then launched into the sky, turning east and disappearing in a low bank of clouds. He was one of the few males of his species left after the battle, and one of only two or three males in my pack. I needed to spend more time with him. We were lost in a sea of women with only each other to commiserate with. I smiled to myself at the image as he winged away.

"Let's move," I said. "We're about to have more company." Already sirens blasted behind us, coming from all directions. And probably with them, the remainder of the ogre mob.

We raced up the stairs, moving as only supernaturals could with speed and stealth unmatched. Even Pamela kept up, all her physical training holding her in good stead. Levi, on the other hand . . . he glanced up at me as the sweat ran down his face. I didn't ask, I just picked him up and threw him over my shoulder. "No, I'm fine," he said, the horror in his voice thick. Of course, I was making him look bad in front of a pretty girl not much younger than him. I shook my head.

"Injuries being healed can take a lot out of you," I said, and he relaxed and let me carry him to the top.

We stopped at the top floor that led out to the viewing platform and restaurant. "No, we have to go higher," Mai said.

From the other side of the door came the pounding of feet and the grunts of ogres. I shared a glance with Lion, but he hadn't heard them yet if his blank stare was any indication.

"Go, all of you!" I pushed them toward the door that led to the mechanical rooms, and I could only pray a door led into the castle on the other side of the Veil.

The door behind me rattled and I grabbed the knob as it turned, forcing it to stay shut. I had to slow the cops and ogres down, to give the rest a head start. Maybe even get Pamela and Mai through the Veil. Because I had no doubt the door to the castle would not keep us safe, and I wasn't about to lead the cops and ogres to Rylee and the babies.

That thought seared through me like a bolt of lightning. I lifted one of the guns I'd taken off the cop from downstairs and held it ready. I flung the door open before they could push their way through. The surprise move caught them off guard, and I was able to grab the cop in the lead by the arm. I dragged him backward and used him as a shield as I sighted down the gun over his shoulder. There were four cops and three ogres. I put the biggest of the ogres into my crosshairs. "You call them all off, or you're going to die and I'll ask your buddy to the right and see if he's smarter than you."

The ogre snarled, showing his teeth. "You killed my brother. I will hunt you down, Wolf."

"Call them off, and you'll get the chance to do that; don't, and . . . well, I think you know how this will end." The thing was, the weight of the gun in my hand told me all I needed to know. It was traditional, with ammo that wouldn't act as it was supposed to. In other words, it wasn't a gun I could depend on, but the ogre in front of me didn't know that.

"I am Vam. I will come for you. I promise you that." He thumped his chest a single time with one fist, and I gave him a nod as I dragged the cop back with me.

"Then I will watch for you, Vam. And you and I can discuss what we're going to do about what happened here and which one of us is going to die as a result of it."

He snarled, but didn't press forward. He wasn't bold like his brother. His brother had been the leader for a reason. Hell, I didn't even remember seeing or smelling Vam in the mob. Those who'd hurt me, those I'd fought, their scents were imprinted in my brain. None of the ogres in the Space Needle had been in the fights.

I backed to the next door, and it yanked open. Lion grabbed me and I shoved the cop toward the ogres and other cops trying to file into the tiny space between doors. They went down in a tangled heap of limbs and curses.

We slammed the door shut behind us and it rattled with the sounds of multiple bullets rocketing into it. Lion and I raced up the final tiny set of stairs to a door that was barely five feet high, and opened into . . . nothing. I peered out and down. There was a slice in the air about twenty feet below the door, a glimmer of light coming through it. A single slice barely big enough for a man to fall through.

I glanced at him, saw the grin on his face as he pushed me. "Shit!"

I fell through the open air and twisted around as the slice in the Veil rushed up to greet me. I blinked, and was through before I truly had time to think about how bad of an idea it was. I landed with a hard thud on the rock of the castle floor in the main courtyard and didn't move fast enough to avoid Lion. He landed on top of me, knocking the wind out of my lungs. I pushed him off and rolled to my feet. Above me, the slice in the Veil was visible, about fifteen feet in the air. High enough to stay out of the way, but if you knew where it was and could leap, you could use it.

Pamela, Levi, and Mai stood to one side.

And Doran strolled up behind them, a grin on his face. The piercing in his bottom lip glinted. "Well, looks like Rylee isn't the only one bringing home new faces."

Mai and Levi spun, but Pamela didn't even flinch. She was used to Doran sneaking up on us when we least expected it. Being a shaman he often had insider information as to what was going to happen. I had no doubt he'd had a vision, or whatever shit he saw when he half closed his eyes to see the future, of us landing in the castle.

"You have a car waiting on the other side?" I asked.

"Better, I have Ophelia. She felt bad leaving you in Seattle," Doran said with a shrug.

Pamela shook her head. "Then why are we standing here?"

I pointed to the slice in the sky above us. "Because there are ogres waiting to come through there and they will follow us home like a stray dog looking for a meal."

She snorted and glanced at Mai. "You said ogres are afraid of heights?"

Mai gave a tight nod. "Yes."

Pamela looked at me. "I had to push her through."

I imagined that didn't go over well. "Then we leave it for now."

"Actually," Lion drawled, his white teeth flashing. "I'd like to sit here and wait on a few of them to come through. Give them a little welcoming party, if you don't mind."

I held a hand out to him and he took it. We hung onto each other, long enough to give each other a nod. I let go and turned my back on him. "Time to go, then."

CHAPTER 12

THE TRIP THROUGH the castle and the mine shaft on the other side was fast with no problems for once. Ophelia took all of us to Bismarck, dropping us off in the backyard of my house.

I hope we are not too late. Ophelia's words were soft inside my head, and full of worry.

"We are not too late," I said, needing to believe the words.

Mai ran ahead without asking, and through the door into the house like she owned the place.

I followed, but Pamela didn't. I paused and looked back at her, but she shook her head. "Go on. I'll come in, in a bit. I want to talk to Marco."

Marco would be hours away, but if she didn't want to talk, that was okay. I suspected her last run looking for supernaturals who'd survived the battle and the pandemic that had swept through both humans and supernaturals had not gone as well as she'd hoped.

Hope was a good thing until it got crushed over and over.

I found myself reluctant to hurry inside the house. Levi shuffled his feet and I understood. We were down to the wire. The chances of all three triplets surviving . . . it was not good. And I knew it. No matter that I chose to believe we still had time.

But I was their father, the only father they knew, and I wasn't going to be a coward now. I made myself walk inside. The back of the house was a mud room/laundry room and I stripped off my clothes and grabbed fresh ones from the laundry basket on top of the dryer.

The smell of sickness permeated everything in the house, from the clean laundry, to the walls as I walked between the doors.

A bustle of activity covered the true desperation of the scene in front of me. Louisa was pouring something into a cup and Mai slammed it back like a shot. Twice more she downed the liquid.

Rylee held Kav in her arms, his skin pale, so very pale. Her eyes lifted to mine. Strain, fear, and fatigue etched into the lines around them. The lack of sleep every mother knew when their child was sick. I walked in and wrapped my arms around them both, holding them up. Giving them what I could in that moment of uncertainty.

Mai held out her hands. "Give him to me. It will help the milk come faster if I hold him."

I released Rylee, but she stood, staring at Mai. I could guess at her thoughts, hell, they were written plainly to see in her eyes. "She's with us, Rylee. I trust her."

"He's my boy," she whispered.

Mai nodded, her eyes filling with tears. "I know. But maybe . . . he can be lucky enough to have two mothers who love him?"

With a hiccup, Rylee handed Kav to Mai. The ogre sat in a kitchen chair and tucked him under her shirt so his face was still visible, but he was against her bare skin. He made a soft fluttering motion with his eyelids and rooted around. She shifted so he could nurse and the little monster . . . he latched on with a ferocity that made Mai wince.

"That's going to hurt when his teeth come in," she said. She stroked his head as his eyelids fluttered open. Rylee sucked in a sharp breath.

"That's the first time he's opened his eyes." Rylee bolted from the room as she spoke, her vampire speed taking her in a flash. She was back before I could respond. Bam was in her arms, as listless as Kav had been only moments before.

She and Mai traded babies, and I took Kav from Rylee. Mai set Bam to her other breast, and he did the same as Kav, latching on in seconds and pulling in the life-giving milk. Kav stared up at me, his color not quite back to normal, but his eyes were bright. He seemed to wink at me and I winked back, finally letting my guard down. I put my head to his and closed my eyes as I breathed him in. One of my boys.

And he was going to live.

Rylee had Rut and again she and Mai did a switch. Mai smiled up her as she took Rut. "They're strong little buggers, aren't they?"

Rylee laughed, but there was a hitch in there. "Yeah, they are." She sat by Mai and stroked Rut's head while he nursed. Bam reached up and touched

Rylee's face and the fear that had been holding us all hostage slowly bled away. Like an abscess lanced, the healing could truly start now.

Kav blinked both eyes, yawned, and stretched before snuggling into my arms. I wasn't worried, though; his heart beat strong, stronger than before I'd left. I held him tightly and sat on the other side of Mai.

She and Rylee were speaking softly, their heads almost touching as they discussed the boys and a nursing schedule. Mai took Kav from me and latched him on to her breast so she was nursing two boys at once. I stood, put a hand on her shoulder, and gave her a squeeze.

"Welcome to the pack, Mai."

Her eyes shot to mine, filling with tears. "Thank you. This . . . this feels like home."

Rylee grinned, her eyes suspiciously wet. "That's because it damn well is. And don't you forget it."

I left them to see Marcella and Zane. Zane saw me first and let out a squeal. I scooped him up and tossed him into the air. His green eyes flashed with nothing short of pure joy and I brought him in close for a hug. He tugged on my hair and tried to jam a finger in my mouth. I laughed and crouched down to Marcella who sat on the floor, Nigel beside her.

She held up her arms, but there was no squeal from her. Just a full certainty that I was there to hold her. I scooped her up in the other arm and kissed her soft cheek.

Rylee was right, again. This was home. This was my pack. And I was the Wolf.

CHAPTER 13

I LEFT THE BABIES in the house, watched over by Rylee's grandparents. There were still a few things that needed dealing with—for one, Levi.

I beckoned for Nigel—the elemental familiar—to follow me out back. Levi still stood outside, as if he didn't dare come in. His eyes shot to mine.

"Are the babies . . . going to make it?"

I clapped my hands onto his shoulders. "We did it. They're going to survive."

He slumped under my hands, and it was only then that I realized how much stock he'd put into coming with me. I tightened my hold on him, just a little. "Thank you, Levi. I could not have survived without you at my side."

He lifted his head slowly. "Really?"

"Really." I let him go. "But I think you should talk to Nigel about what you should be able to do, and what you might have yet to learn about your bloodline. Maybe go inside and you can talk to your sister, too."

He nodded and Nigel grunted. "They're part-bloods, different than half-breeds, Wolf. What do you expect they can do?"

I lifted an eyebrow at Levi and he flicked his hands at the jackal. Water exploded up from under the smaller canine, throwing him into the air. He yelped as he twisted twenty feet up.

"Okay, okay! I get the point, you're stronger than we thought. Shit, what is the mother goddess up to now?"

Levi lowered him with a grin, and a not so subtle look over his shoulder to where Pamela sat in the vine-covered gazebo. She wasn't watching him, much to his obvious disappointment as his shoulders slumped. Pamela's eyes were on the sky, searching for something. Presumably Marco, but I thought now that perhaps that was just a ruse.

"Go on." I pushed Levi gently toward the house. He and Nigel disappeared inside and the last thing I heard was Nigel grumping.

"You know, things used to not change. All of a sudden, everyone's breaking the rules. Nothing's holding to old patterns."

I wondered at his words and couldn't help the saying that slipped from my lips. "Rules were made to be broken."

Pamela turned to me. "Do you really believe that?"

I sat next to her and slung an arm over her shoulder. "I think the rules of our world are ever changing. That means sometimes we break them without realizing. But you didn't ask that just because, did you?"

Her lips tightened and she shook her head. "No, I didn't. I . . . I have to go away, Liam."

I stared at her, seeing her actual age versus her physical age. "For how long?"

Her eyes shot to mine. "You aren't going to stop me?"

I leaned back and stared at the sky, as if the answers truly could be found there. "No. I understand the need to have space, and both Rylee and I have struggled to figure out how we fit into this new version of our world. So if you need to go, just promise me one thing."

Her blue eyes were serious as they locked onto mine. "What's that?"

I pulled her into a hug. "Come home to us, wolf cub. Always come home to us."

With a sob, she hugged me. "Always. I will always come home." And then she stood. "Tell Rylee . . . I don't know what, that I'm sorry—"

I gave her a wink. "Don't worry about Rylee. She knows, Pam. She's always known you belonged with us."

She sat there another minute, as if she didn't quite want to leave either.

"The world is coming apart at the seams, Liam, I can feel it in my blood." Her words were soft, barely flitting to me even with the short space between us.

I gave a slow nod. "I know. I can feel it too. There is more danger coming our way."

She closed her eyes and a tear slipped from the corner of one. "That's why I have to go. I have . . . to be strong enough. I can't learn from anyone here."

I smiled and tugged her to my side, giving her

another hug. "You don't have to explain it to me, little witch. I trust your instincts."

She blinked up at me. "Thank you."

Gently, she pushed my arm off from over her shoulders and she took a few steps back. Her throat bobbed and she sniffed a couple of times. With great care she lifted a hand to me, a final farewell.

With a tiny sob, she spun and ran from the yard, her bright blonde hair floating on the breeze behind her.

I swallowed down a sudden spurt of fear for the young witch. I wanted to tell her to stay, that whatever she was looking for was here. But I knew better, I'd seen it in Rylee, and I'd seen it in myself. The battle with Orion had changed us all, and in that change we all needed to figure out who we were now that the imminent destruction of the world was no longer at hand.

On her back and under the long cloak she wore I saw the outline of a sword handle. If the wind hadn't caught her hair and pulled it away, I would never have even noticed it.

"Be safe, Pamela. And come home to us when you find what you're looking for. When you finally realize you were already strong enough."

Turning away, I walked back to the house. Inside, the tension was gone, the smell of sickness was fading. I stood in the kitchen and listened to those who were my pack.

Nigel was speaking to Belinda and Levi, his voice

muffled through the walls, but here and there I picked up a word. Elementals. Power. Training. That was good. If he could help them with some training, they could be as much a part of keeping our pack together as Pamela, or Eve.

Through the house I walked, checking on everyone. Marcella and Zane were asleep in their crib, their hands clasped. I ran a hand over each of their heads, needing to just feel their soft skin for a moment. To know that they were safe. Healthy.

I backed out of the room and followed the sound of Mai's heartbeat. She sat in what had been my office. It had been quickly converted into a bedroom. She lay on a mattress on the floor with the three triplets next to her. Well, to be fair, one was curled in her arms and the other two slept to either side.

"How are you doing, Mai?"

She nodded, and a sad smile crossed her lips. "Tired. Thirsty."

I went and got a large pitcher of water and a glass from the kitchen and brought them back to her. She took the cup and downed the entire glass. I poured her another and she drank it halfway down. "Thanks." She put the cup down on a side table set up next to the makeshift bed. "Did you really mean what you said, about me belonging? About being a part of your pack?"

I nodded. "Yes, I knew it within minutes of meeting you."

Her eyelids fluttered as if clearing away sleep. "How?"

Crouching beside her, I reached out and touched Bam, as he was closest to me. "Is Mai your full name?"

She rolled her eyes. "How did you know it wasn't?"

My ears twitched as Rylee stepped into the doorway behind me, listening. "What is your full name, Mai?"

"It's stupid, I hate it."

I laughed softly. "Tell me anyway."

"Well." Mai shifted in her spot so she was sitting up better. "I have to preface this. My mother broke tradition by giving me a four-letter name. But the word in ogre tradition means 'life's warrior'."

She was stalling, but not for the reason I'd first thought. "So your name . . ."

Mai sighed. "Ma-il. Pronounced phonetically. But I was teased as 'mail call' all the time as you can imagine. Which is why I dropped the last letter."

Rylee snorted. "People are shitty."

Mai nodded. But I wasn't done.

"Mai. Spell your name backwards for me." I smiled, looking forward to Rylee and Mai seeing what I saw. Seeing just how serendipitous things were in our world.

She shrugged. "L-I-A-M." Her jaw dropped as she spoke, her eyes widened to round saucers and she stared at me. "Holy shit."

Behind me, Rylee sucked in a breath. "Holy shit indeed."

I stood, satisfied that they both believed as I did that Mai belonged with us. "Good night, Mai. Sleep well and know that you do belong with us."

I stepped back. Rylee leaned in. "And if you need help with the triplets tonight—"

"I'll be fine," she waved at us. "Go and rest. Tomorrow is soon enough to figure out a schedule."

I took Rylee by the hand and led her to our bedroom, then through to the master bath. I flicked on the shower as hot as it would go, stripped and helped Rylee out of her clothes. I didn't want sex, I just wanted to hold her.

"Liam, are you okay?" She touched a hand to my face, her eyes full of concern.

I stepped into the shower and tugged her in with me. The hot water sluiced over our skin, washing away the last two days. Washing away the last of the fears that had resided so deep in my heart I'd not even realized they'd been there.

I wrapped my arms around her and held her tight, skin to skin, heart to heart. "Yeah, I'm good now that I'm home. With you."

We stood there together, just hanging onto each other, baptized anew in each other's arms.

I pulled back a little so I could look in her eyes. They were clear, no residue of the uncertainty she'd had before. "You good?"

"I'm fucking amazing. You saved them, Liam, and our family is whole again."

I drew in a slow breath and shook my head. "Not yet."

She frowned. "What do you mean, not yet?"

I flicked the water off and grabbed two towels, tossing one to her.

"We need to talk about Pam."

CHAPTER 15

PAMELA

I ALL BUT RAN from the backyard. Liam's gentle understanding almost had me spilling my secrets to him. I want to tell him that I'd found someone to train me not only in the possible, but the impossible, too. But that I was afraid as well.

Not that I didn't trust the one who was going to train me, but if I was wrong about him . . . I couldn't bear the thought of him somehow using my family, of hurting them.

Still, I couldn't deny that what he offered was far too tempting for me to just walk away from. I would train with him, learn all I could, and if he lied . . .

"If I lie to you, what then?"

I spun around to see the handsome man I'd met on my last run with Marco. He had jet-black hair and bright blue eyes, his smile was easy, and he had seemed kind. He wore clothes that reminded me somehow of Lark, the elemental who'd helped us face the demon horde.

Even with all those things, my instincts screamed at me to be cautious, that this man could destroy me if I was not very careful.

I made myself keep my face even, without emotion. I arched an eyebrow, thinking of Rylee. "You'll pay dearly if you lie to me. You said you could tell me how to open the Veil, that I could bring Frank back."

Frank, my first love, had died to save me. I could not forget his sacrifice, and I knew I had to do everything I could to give him a second chance. The way Liam had a second chance and had come back to Rylee.

The dark-haired man nodded, his lips downturned, but it was false in his concern over my words. The humor in his eyes offset the frown on his lips.

"Well, then let us work on bringing your Frank back. Did you bring the payment I require?"

From my back, I pulled out the sword that Lark had made for Rylee. A powerful weapon that could do things no weapon should be able to. Like slice through the Veil. But no matter how I'd used it, I had not been able to get it to slice the Veil as it had done for Rylee and Lark.

Which was why I needed the man in front of me.

I held the weapon for a moment, knowing that Rylee would be pissed as a housecat stuck in a rainstorm . . . but to learn what I needed to learn, I would betray her in this. I started to hand the sword over to him, then pulled it back at the last second.

"You can have it after you teach me what I want to know . . . Raven. You've seen it, and I will hold onto it until I'm satisfied with what I've learned."

He laughed. "You're smarter than the average witch, I'll give you that. Especially considering your age. What are you, fifteen?"

I nodded, surprised that he guessed so close. Most people thought I was older.

He winked at me. "I bet you take after your father."

I shrugged and put the sword away, strapping it to my back in a sheath patterned after Rylee's. "I wouldn't know, I never met him."

"Well, then I think we should change that. Why don't I introduce you to him?"

I couldn't help the shake in my hands, and couldn't keep my face from the race of emotions that whipped through me. "You know my father?"

Raven laughed, and put his hands on his hips. "I know him. Are you ready to meet him and learn all I have to teach you, little witch?"

I lifted my chin, knowing I was facing a man who could indeed teach me, or kill me depending on his mood.

But there was no way I was letting Frank rot. Not when I had a chance to bring him back.

I steeled myself, and took the plunge into the unknown.

"I'm ready."

Acknowledgments

You'd think I'd run out of people to thank after this many books but the reality is each book takes a team, and a support network to bring it about. From my amazing editors (Tina Winograd, Shannon Page, Stephanie Erickson) to my fantastic ARC team (who always manage to find a few more typos for me to fix!) to my always amazing right hand gal, Lysa Lessieur, you all make this writing job continue to feel like an adventure of epic proportions.

Thank you from the bottom of my heart for sticking out the rough patches with me, you all deserve medals for laying in the trenches beside me as we fight side by side with the characters we all know and love.

Here's to teamwork.

And my very own pack of kick-ass women.

AUTHORS NOTE

Thanks for reading "LIAM (The Rylee Adamson Epilogues, Book 2)". I truly hope you enjoyed this glimpse into Rylee and the gang's lives after the Final Battle. I heard you when you asked for more Rylee, and the characters ended up having more to say as well. If you loved this book, one of the best things you can do is leave a review for it. Amazon is where I sell the majority of my work, so if I can only ask for one place for reviews that would be it it – but feel free to spread the word on all retailers.

Again, thank you for coming on this ride with me, I hope we'll take many more together. The rest of The Rylee Adamson Novels, along with my other novels, are available in both ebook and paperback format on all major retailers. You will find purchase links on my website at www.shannonmayer.com.

Enjoy!

ABOUT THE AUTHOR

Shannon Mayer lives in the southwestern tip of Canada with her husband, dog, cats, horse, and cows. When not writing she spends her time staring at immense amounts of rain, herding old people (similar to herding cats) and attempting to stay out of trouble. Especially that last is difficult for her.

She is the *USA Today* Bestselling author of the The Rylee Adamson Novels, The Elemental Series, The Nevermore Trilogy, A Celtic Legacy series and several contemporary romances. Please visit her website for more information on her novels.

http://www.shannonmayer.com/

Ms. Mayer's books can be found at these retailers:

Amazon
iBooks
Barnes & Noble
Kobo
Google Play
Smashwords